UP THE CREEK

Natalie Hyde

Cover by Julie McLaughlin

Scholastic Canada Ltd.
Toronto New York London Auckland Sydney
Mexico City New Delhi Hong Kong Buenos Aires

Scholastic Canada Ltd.
604 King Street West, Toronto, Ontario M5V 1E1, Canada

Scholastic Inc.
557 Broadway, New York, NY 10012, USA

Scholastic Australia Pty Limited
PO Box 579, Gosford, NSW 2250, Australia

Scholastic New Zealand Limited
Private Bag 94407, Botany, Manukau 2163, New Zealand

Scholastic Children's Books
Euston House, 24 Eversholt Street, London NW1 1DB, UK

www.scholastic.ca

Library and Archives Canada Cataloguing in Publication
Title: Up the creek / Natalie Hyde ; cover by Julie McLaughlin.
Names: Hyde, Natalie, 1963- author.
Identifiers: Canadiana (print) 20200282042 | Canadiana (ebook) 20200282069 | ISBN 9781443175746 (softcover) | ISBN 9781443175753 (ebook)
Classification: LCC PS8615.Y33 U6 2021 | DDC jC813/.6—dc23

Cover by Julie McLaughlin

6 5 4 3 2 1 Printed in Canada 114 21 22 23 24 25

For Craig, who is always ready for an adventure.

CHAPTER 1

MINE TOO!

I found my grandfather's toe lying in some liquid at the bottom of a Mason jar. I knew it was his because Dad once told me Granddad lost a toe chopping wood. Plus, it's gross enough to keep your own toe, but I couldn't even imagine what sort of person would keep someone else's. The toe was all blackened and surprisingly long. The toenail was even still on it. I almost gagged. I had stumbled across it tucked up in the rafters when I was poking around the old, decrepit cabin on our claim outside Dawson City, Yukon.

"By Jove, this is quite a mess, heh?" Neils said, blocking the light of the doorway with his broad shoulders. If your only parent has been sent to county jail for getting mixed up with some stolen goods and you have to have a foster father, you want one like Neils: a six-foot-tall Norwegian with hair that looks like he cuts it with a chainsaw. No one messes with you when you've got a Viking on your side. "It'll take some doing to set this right."

I had to agree with him. Granddad's old cabin had been abandoned for years and years, and I think even when it was new, it was just thrown together in a hurry. From the old pictures I had seen, miners were eager to get on with pulling a fortune in gold out of the ground — they didn't care what kind of house they lived in.

But I did. I was going to try to fix it up for when my dad came and we started mining our claim. *Our claim.* I loved the sound of that.

I didn't even know where I'd begin. Most of the wooden shelves had fallen or were hanging by one nail. Rusty cans and broken bottles were scattered on the ground. The slats of the small bed tucked in a corner had snapped in two, and the thin mattress hanging off it seemed to be a motel for mice, judging from the stuffing strewn about.

"It'll be fine once it's fixed up," I said. With summer vacation on, I could work on it most days.

Neils raised his eyebrows. "Look, Chris, I know how much you went through to get up here and get your grandfather's claim back, but fixing up this cabin is just the beginning. It's a lot of work to get a mine up and running . . . not to mention making a profit. A lot of people never make a go of it."

I didn't answer. I had never told Neils what I left behind, but one thing was for sure — the city was no place for Dad and me. We had been hours away from being evicted from our tiny, crappy apartment that was way too close to the bars my dad snuck away to, spending our rent money on beer. This gold claim was our ticket to a new life; the kind of life other people took for granted, with money to pay your bills so the electricity was never turned off, a fridge full of food for the whole month and even new shoes when the bottoms wore through your old ones and your feet got soaked when it rained.

"I know," I told Neils. "But if I can work on the cabin, that will give my dad a head start on getting the mine going."

Neils huffed like he wasn't getting through to me. I turned around and pretended to be sizing up the work the cabin needed so I wouldn't have to continue the conversation. I didn't care if we had to drink water from the creek, eat nothing but ramen noodles for a year or even use a tree for our bathroom — we were *never* going back.

"We better get going. Anna has supper ready, I think," he said, walking out the door. Neils's wife, Anna, might be a softie when it came to chores but she was a stickler for punctuality. We both knew that if we were late for a meal, we might not get any.

As I put the toe jar back on the rafter, a small packet fell to the ground. It just looked like a bit of brown paper tied with a string. I almost didn't open it, but then I figured something that had been hidden behind a gross jar of toe might be interesting. I untied the string, and the folds of paper crackled as I peeled them back. There, in the gloom of the cabin, glowed a piece of deep yellow rock about the size of a cough drop.

I couldn't take my eyes off it. It was heavier than you'd think for something that small, and as I closed my fist around it, I knew it was gold. It must have been my granddad's — it was in his cabin. I opened my fist again. A gold nugget. I knew it. I knew my granddad was right. The Dearing claim *did* have a pay streak. It was like my grandfather was talking to me, telling me everything was going to be all right.

I put the nugget in my pocket and pulled the door closed behind me — gently, because from the sounds of the hinges, one good yank and it would come right off. I wished I could get started on the cabin right away — my dad would need somewhere to stay. I hoped he wouldn't take too long to come or we would miss the mining season.

Gold mining in the Yukon is only possible for

a few months during the short summers, so you have to get started as soon as it turns warm and go right until the snow comes. But so far not even one shovelful of dirt on our claim had been moved. Nothing could start until my dad was released from jail and got up here. I guess it's not a good thing that there are so many criminals the jails were stuffed to bursting. But an overcrowded county jail did mean that people with less serious charges, like my dad, were getting released sooner. It seems the only time we Dearings have good luck is when prison is involved.

I had only heard from Dad once in the few weeks I'd been in Dawson. He wasn't really regular with stuff like phone calls, but it worried me just the same. At our meeting the week before, I had asked Mrs. Child Protective Services, also known as Mrs. Olsen, if she had talked to him lately.

"Yes, briefly," she had answered.

I waited for her to go on, but she was suddenly very preoccupied with paperwork on her desk.

"Well?"

"Well, what?"

"Is he okay? Does he have a release date?" I almost added "Did he ask about me?" but changed my mind. If he hadn't, it would sting too much.

"No, he doesn't have a firm date. There are . . . complications."

"Like what?"

She finally looked at me. "Nothing for you to be concerned about. He'll get out when he gets out. Meanwhile, let's talk about school in the fall."

I barely heard what she said after that. The word *complications* made my stomach hurt. Was she hiding some bad news from me?

* * *

After chicken and dumplings, Neils and I went out to the dog yard in the clearing behind the house to feed his sled dogs. In the few weeks I'd been here, they'd gotten pretty used to me. Bullet was my favourite. Neils said Bullet got his name because he liked to go fast. His floppy ears and the way he tilted his head to the side when I talked to him reminded me a bit of Bandit, the stray I left behind at our old apartment building. When I left Ontario to come to the Yukon and get the Dearing claim back, I didn't really think about the fact that I probably would never see Bandit again.

"How fast does Bullet go?" I asked Neils.

"So fast that you feel like the sled isn't even touching the ground and the wind burns your cheeks."

I couldn't wait to try it.

Anna came out to dump the scraps from supper in her compost bin.

"So, when are you planning to start mining, Chris?" she asked.

I shrugged.

She gave Neils a look.

Neils cleared his throat. "I think we had better start with the basics. I'll drive you down to our claim tomorrow," he said.

"Drive? I thought *this* was your claim," I said, looking around.

Neils shook his head. "This spot was cleared out years ago. No, I've got a block of claims a few kilometres south of here on Badger Creek."

"A block? How many claims are there?"

"Oh, about sixteen or so."

"Why do you have so many?"

"Well, to get the yardage we need to make a profit, we chew through the dirt pretty fast."

I suddenly began to worry about my family's claim. It was tiny compared to Neils's. Maybe it wasn't big enough for a pay streak. Maybe my granddad had already found all the gold on it and all that was left was the nugget I found. And then it dawned on me that even if there *was* still gold, I had no idea where to start searching for it. My dad never said what Granddad's hint was, and I sure hoped he remembered, otherwise we'd be worse off than we were before — if that was even possible.

CHAPTER 2

A FLASH OF LIGHTNING

The next morning I was up early. Well, early for me but not for Neils.

"What time would I have to get up to beat Neils?" I asked Anna, as she handed me some orange juice.

She laughed. "The only ones up before Neils are the dawn chorus."

"The what?"

"The birds that sing as the sun comes up — chickadees, warblers, sparrows. They're the only ones that see Neils in the morning. *I* don't even get up that early."

"Where is he?"

"He's out feeding the dogs."

Those dogs were fed better than I had been for years when it was just me and my dad. But thanks to Anna's cooking, I could now wear my jeans without a belt holding them up. I wolfed down my eggs and hash browns so I wouldn't keep Neils waiting. I was excited to see his gold operation. When I climbed into Neils's blue truck, he said, "We need to make a stop at the junkyard first. I need some parts for our old D10."

"D10?"

"Our Cat."

I stared at him with a blank look on my face. He used a cat for gold mining?

"Caterpillar," he said, noticing my confusion.

"Oh, right." I said slowly, wondering if he was teasing me.

"It's a brand of bulldozer."

I was still confused. "Um, Neils? Aren't you supposed to dig *down* into the ground for gold?"

"First you have to get to the gold-bearing soil," he explained. "You have to scrape away all the topsoil with a dozer. *Then* you dig up the dirt and process it."

"Oh."

"Sometimes pay dirt is five, six metres down. And most might be frozen still, even in summer. You need a sluice box to filter the gold out of the dirt. The tailings need to be taken care of. And then when you are finished mining, you have to return the land to the way it was."

My head started to spin. When my dad had told me that gold mining needed equipment, I thought he meant picks, shovels and buckets. But heavy-duty trucks? Sluices? Tailings? I had never heard of those things. I'm sure the old-timers hadn't either. Didn't they just use one of those pans in a creek?

I said nothing to Neils. I'm sure this was the way big companies did it, but we just didn't have that kind of cash. We were going to have to start small.

We bounced along in the pickup truck toward Dawson, past massive rippled piles of stones, and turned right on a dirt road just outside of town. My teeth rattled in my head from the potholes and the spray of tan mud hitting the windows.

"Only two states of the roads in Dawson," Neils said. "Dusty or muddy."

Around a bend I could see a massive structure rising above the trees. It looked like a building with grey plank walls and several small windows, but sticking out one end was a huge crane-like arm holding a row of metal buckets, and out the other end was some sort of tunnel pointing into the air. Boards, trim and sheet metal were missing from the upper levels, and the whole thing looked like it was ready to collapse. This didn't look like any junkyard I had ever seen before.

"What *is* that?" I asked.

"Dredge Number Two."

"Number two? There were more of these?"

"About twenty-four of them at the height of gold dredging."

"It's for finding gold?"

"Yup. That bucket line dug up the ground at the front and dumped it inside to be sluiced, then the tailings came out the stacker."

My heart sank. This was even more complicated than Neils's operation.

As we got closer, rusted cars were lined up all along the road, and to our right was a tower of hubcaps that looked like it was ready to topple. The yard in front of the dredge was a labyrinth of stuff. Piles of boilers and barrels over here, pipes and bicycle frames over there.

"A guy could get lost in there," I said, pointing at the junkyard.

"I heard of that happening," Neils said, pulling up to the dredge. "They say Jerry Stuart went in there as a young boy looking for a new wheel for his bike and came out with a full beard."

As we got out of the pickup, a door at the bottom of the dredge swung open and a man came out. He quickly walked over to us and then kept shifting his weight from foot to foot. He looked ready to run a marathon. He was skinny enough for it too.

"Hiya, Gord. Is Lucy about?" Neils asked, looking around nervously.

Gord jerked a thumb back toward the dredge. "Aye, she's inside having her breakfast."

Neils looked relieved.

"And who's this?" Gord asked, smiling at me.

"This here's Chris. He's staying with Anna and me for a while."

Gord gave me a bit of a nod and a smile. I gave a small wave.

"I need some gaskets for the D10," Neils said. "You got any to fit?"

"Should have. Let me check."

Gord scurried off toward the maze of piles. His hands were twitching the whole time and he kept glancing at the sky. Before long he disappeared, his running shoes not making a sound on the ground.

"Shouldn't he be wearing safety boots in there?" I asked, looking at the metal shards, nails and screws littering the ground.

"You won't catch Flash Gordon wearing anything with metal in it," Neils said, glancing every now and then at the open doorway into the dredge.

Flash Gordon? Like the superhero? Another lucky person with a cool nickname. My best friend, Shard Kent, has a superhero name too.

Her first name means a jagged piece of glass and her last name is the same as Superman's alter ego, Clark Kent. How neat is that? She used to tell everyone she was Superman's cousin. I'm not sure she isn't.

"Why won't he wear metal?"

"Because he's been struck by lightning three times. He won't wear anything with metal on it — no zippers, no rivets, no metal buttons and no steel plates in his shoes."

Maybe not so lucky.

And maybe not the best place for him to work either.

Out of nowhere came an ear-splitting shriek, a slapping sound and a flurry of movement from the door of the dredge.

"Quick!" Neils yelled. "Get back in the truck!"

I didn't need to be told twice. I flung open the door and hopped in, then slammed it behind me, terrified.

"What is it?" I asked.

"It's Lucy," Neils whispered.

My eyes swung back to the doorway. Out waddled the most enormous Canada goose I had ever seen. She marched right up to Neils's side of the truck and started squawking and beating her wings on his door.

"Lucy?" I repeated.

"She's Gord's guard goose."

I thought I had seen it all with an onion-loving moose. When I first came to stake our claim, I was treed by an angry mama moose. Shard's idea to ward her off using onions was a joke, because the moose loved them and chased me all over to get more. I still haven't really forgiven Shard for that. And now a guard goose? She was even angrier than that mama moose. Would we be trapped in here forever?

"Settle down, Lucy. It's only Neils," Flash Gordon said, reappearing from behind a pile of refrigerators and freezers with the doors taken off. Lucy gave one final, disgusted honk and waddled away.

"You can come out now," he said to Neils, a smile pulling at the corners of his mouth.

Neils opened the door again and got out slowly, looking in the direction Lucy had gone. I climbed out too. But I left the door open for a quick retreat.

"These should fit," Gord said, handing the D10 parts to Neils.

"How much do I owe you?"

"Come inside. I have to look it up."

Neils closed the door behind him while they went in the dredge, which left me alone in the junkyard with an angry goose on the loose. I leaned against the truck, soaking up the warm sun and listening for the slap of webbed feet. I heard nothing, so I took a chance and began poking around. Maybe there was something here to upgrade the cabin from pretty rough to sort of livable. Like a toaster oven. Or a second chair.

I had found an old spotlight I was sure my dad could turn into a cool light fixture when I heard it . . . *gleep, gleep, gleep*. Lucy was coming. I backed up and turned to run. Too late! Lucy was right in front of me. Her neck lengthened and her beady black eyes were fixed on my throat. She spread her wings and took one step toward me. I dodged sideways, still facing her. She hissed. I ran for the truck. She came charging after me, wings flapping. I made it to the open door, jumped in, and slammed it shut. I could hear her beating on the door.

"Lucy! Down!"

The banging stopped and Lucy waddled away as Gord came over to the truck — followed by Neils, who looked like he was using Gord as a shield. I put the window down a bit.

"Popcorn," Gord said, glancing at the sky and not touching the truck.

"Pardon?"

"Lucy loves popcorn. No butter, though. She

needs to watch her weight. Bring some popcorn and she'll leave you alone. She'll remember you too."

I nodded as if I understood. What was it with animals and food up here? Moose loving onions, geese wanting popcorn. Was there a bear somewhere that demanded nachos?

Neils climbed in the truck, throwing the gaskets on the bench between us. He started it up and turned it around.

"Where does Gord live?" I asked Neils, looking around for a shack or trailer.

"In the dredge."

I looked back out the rear window.

"Isn't it full of metal machinery? For gold mining, I mean."

"Once was. But he took it all out, piece by piece. That's how the junkyard started. His yard was full of scrap metal from the dredge."

"Isn't that kind of dangerous for someone who's a target for lightning?" I asked.

Neils shrugged. "Maybe he thinks the lightning won't find him among all those piles of metal."

I said nothing. But someone should tell Flash Gordon that if bad luck wants to find you, it will, no matter where you hide.

CHAPTER 3

DREDGING UP THE PAST

Neils headed back in the direction of Cottonwood Creek Road but kept on going past both his house and my granddad's claim.

"How far is your claim?"

"A couple more kilometres."

The road got rougher the farther we went. Then Neils turned off the dirt road to a dirt lane. We were really bouncing now as we went over ruts. I was glad I had a seat belt to keep me from smacking my head on the roof. Finally he slowed and turned through a stand of birches. In a clearing ahead of us was a huge yellow-and-black machine sitting up on a pile of dirt and rocks.

"That's our sluice," Neils said, pointing. "We call it Little Hornet."

A front-end loader carrying a load of dirt rumbled up to Little Hornet and dumped it into the top. The machine swallowed its meal, then spit it out the other side onto a conveyor belt. Water sprayed over the dirt and rocks, allowing the smaller bits to fall below, and then the conveyor belt rolled the garbage stones out the other end.

"Do you have to use a sluice to mine gold?" I asked. I hadn't pictured a sluice as being this big. And big equals expensive. I wasn't even sure we could afford shovels and pans, let alone a machine like this.

"Only way to get enough gold. The days of dipping your pan into a creek and finding big nuggets ended with the gold rush in 1899."

"How much do sluices cost?" I asked.

"Oh, new about $15,000, $20,000 for one like this."

I felt the blood run out of my face. The one time my dad was able to phone, I talked up how this was our new start and we were going to be able to make some money. He once told me it wasn't cheap to set up a gold-mining operation, and now I knew what he meant. But we had made do with practically no money before. You just have to be inventive. When my dad finally made it up here, there's no way he would have ready cash to buy anything big like this. We would have to think of something else. For a second I thought of the gold nugget, but Granddad must have kept it for a reason, so I wasn't ready to part with it.

"Can you get some second-hand?" I asked Neils.

"You mean for the Dearing claim?"

I nodded.

"I have some connections. I'm sure we can find something in your price range."

I hoped Neils understood our price range was from zero dollars to free.

Neils continued driving past the sluice until we came to another clearing. Two parked trailers faced each other across an open space with a firepit and lawn chairs in the middle. He parked the truck and we got out.

"Who lives here?" I asked.

"Oh, these are Leo's and Dave's luxury accommodations for the mining season," he said, chuckling at his own joke. "They only come up for the summer. Dave lives in Edmonton and Leo goes back to Vancouver in the winter. Wimps." Then he laughed again. "Only tough guys like us can make it through the winters, right?" He punched me lightly on the shoulder.

I smiled and nodded, but inside I was wondering about what lay ahead. What made it so bad that grown men wouldn't stay? I mean, I was used to snow and cold, so how much worse could it get? I didn't ask, though. I would stay through any kind of winter if my dad was here and we were making money on the claim. It was torture to live so close to my granddad's claim and not be able to work it.

"I want to show you something," Neils said, motioning for me to follow him to a domed shelter with a white plastic roof. Inside were wooden tables with gold pans, magnets and metal trays on them. In a corner was a pile of tall rubber boots. And at the far end was a strange, spiralled round tray sitting on an angle. Water came out a small tube and sprayed over the black dirt going around and around on it.

"What is that thing?" I said, walking over to it.

"This here," Neils said, "is a concentrator."

"Uh-huh."

"Come look at the back of it."

I got closer and looked behind the weird spiral tray. At the back was a margarine tub with a big black rock in it.

"Cool," I said, not having any idea what I was looking at.

Neils laughed. He turned off the machine and lifted the tub. He took out the dark rock and showed me what was hiding underneath — a layer of glittering sand. At least it looked like sand, but it practically glowed, even in the dim light of the shelter. No one had to tell me twice . . . it was gold.

"They're so small," I said, running a finger through the grains.

"This is the fine gold," Neils said. "We use this

machine to get the really small flakes out of the concentrate from the sluice. This pile of yellow is what we work for. This is the stuff that drives men mad with gold fever."

"Doesn't look like much," I said. Each one was so tiny compared to the nugget I found in Granddad's cabin. I hadn't shown the nugget to Neils. He would probably tell me there was no proof it came from Granddad's claim, just like I was sure everyone else would. But I knew differently.

"No? Well, in this tub here is about twenty ounces. Right now, that's worth almost $40,000."

My mouth fell open. I looked back in the margarine tub. The twenty ounces of gold dust looked like the amount of powdered cheese you get in a box of macaroni and cheese dinner. Forty thousand dollars? My dad and I could live on that for a year! Maybe two if we ate more boxed macaroni and cheese.

"How long did it take to get this much?" I asked, still mesmerized by it.

"It's about a week's worth of sluicing."

"Oh. How long would it take without a sluice?"

Neils laughed. "A lot longer. Look, I have to help Dave with these parts. Why don't you grab some of these rubber boots, and Leo will show you how to pan properly in the creek over there."

You know, decked out in rubber boots up to

my knees, bending over the creek with a battered metal pan, I felt this connection to my granddad. Maybe it was because he was in the same pose in the old photo of him Dad kept in the living room of our apartment. The photo I brought north with me. I wondered if Granddad had panned in this very spot. I could feel confidence building. He had found gold — we would too. Even if it took us a little longer than these big operations.

"You must be Chris," a man with shaggy brown hair said, coming over to me. "I'm Leo."

Leo turned out to be pretty laid back and seemed happy to show me how to pan for gold.

"You go with Neils to the junkyard to get the parts?" Leo asked me, still washing dirt and gravel from his pan.

"Yeah."

"Must've been strange."

I thought of Lucy, the popcorn-loving guard goose; Flash Gordon, the human lightning magnet; and the towering piles of rusty metal. Which strange part was he referring to?

"Sure was."

"Never thought a Dearing would dare take a step on that property again," he said, chuckling.

You know how you get that feeling you're about to get some bad news? Yeah, well that feeling raced through me like a flooding river of dread.

"Um. Why is that?"

Leo gave me a surprised look. "The dredge."

I shook my head.

"Your granddad worked on it."

I straightened up. "I didn't know he worked on a dredge."

Leo nodded. "Oh yes. By the time he got here, well, lots of miners actually, all the good claims had been taken and mined out. But the dredges working in the river valleys that were owned by the big companies kept the gold flowing for years."

I had no idea. Dad had never mentioned his father working on a dredge. I thought he only worked on his claims. "So, he worked on Dredge Number Two? For how long?"

Leo snorted. "Until the theft."

"What theft?"

Leo looked at me with a confused expression. "On the dredge. When he was accused of stealing . . . Surely your dad told . . . Oh, sorry. Me an' my big mouth. I thought you knew."

Leo turned a bit red, made some excuse about having to check the sluice, and left. I was so shocked I couldn't react.

Granddad? Accused of robbery? Just when I thought I was pulling the Dearing name out of the muck, something else came along to drag us back down.

CHAPTER 4

FAMILIAR FACES

The Dawson City General Store was hopping for a Friday morning. I was helping Anna with the shopping while Neils took a candle holder he had found buried on his claim to the Trading Post.

"Why doesn't he just keep it?" I asked Anna, as we navigated the narrow aisles that had products stuffed into every available space. Seaweed and couscous hung on hooks by the spice shelf. Bins and baskets of fruits and vegetables battled for every inch of the aisles, leaving almost no room to get through. The murmur of voices coming from every corner of the store was punctuated with the squeak of shopping-cart wheels.

"Neils takes the better stuff to Ian to sell," Anna said. "Some things can turn out to be pretty valuable."

I'm not sure why Neils thought this candle

holder would be valuable. It just looked like a spoon that had been bent in a circle. It always surprised me how people long ago found ways to make things with the stuff they had lying around.

"Bacon or sausage?" Anna suddenly asked me.

I didn't know what it was for, but the answer was simple. "Bacon." The answer is always bacon.

Then I headed to the snack aisle because Anna said I could pick a treat for our movie night tonight. It was a toss-up between barbecue chips and potato sticks. I was staring at the bags, trying to decide, when someone bumped into my arm.

"Sorry," a voice said.

I turned to see a familiar face. "Vinnie!" I said. "How are you? I haven't seen you since we first got here."

Vinnie towered over me, his lanky arms awkwardly holding a wire basket full of items. I had missed his goofy smile and always-optimistic attitude, not to mention his muffins. What would I have done if he and Shard hadn't rescued me, Fiona and her broken motorbike, then brought us up to Dawson in his food truck? Not everyone in the world would drop everything and take their business on the road because their niece's friend needed help. If Vinnie hadn't rescued my mission to regain the Dearing claim, who knows where I'd be right now. I didn't want to think about it.

"Chris! How's it going? If I had known I was going to bump into you, I would have brought you some day-old muffins. I've got lots," he added, with a grimace.

"Oh. Is your Muffin Man business not too good?"

"Some of my regular customers are saying they need to cut down because they're putting on weight. Dr. Bolton has my picture up on his waiting room wall with a big red line through it. So, I'm trying to come up with a diet muffin . . ." He raised his basket to show me the ingredients in it: cabbage, grapefruit and lima beans. ". . . But it's a challenge."

I couldn't imagine even Vinnie's baking skills turning lima beans into a yummy muffin.

"I'm going to drop some Lemon Liftoff muffins to Flash Gordon this afternoon," he continued. "He's about the only person in the Klondike who isn't complaining about his pants fitting."

"I didn't know you delivered."

"Well, this is a special case. Gord won't ride in a car. Or on a bike. So, he couldn't get to the food truck very easily. I felt sorry for him."

"Have you ever been to the junkyard before?" I asked.

Vinnie shook his head. "Weather's just settled down enough for me to use my motorbike."

"You have a motorbike? When did that happen?"

"Fiona hooked me up with a friend who had one for sale. It's a rebuild, but it gets me around."

It didn't surprise me that Fiona had connections when it came to motorbikes. Her Italian Ducati motorcycle was legendary.

"Well, if you're going to Flash Gordon's and you value your life, take popcorn," I said.

"What?"

"For his guard goose, Lucy. Apparently she'll leave you alone if you bring her popcorn."

"Thanks for the tip!" Vinnie said, doing a little hop. "I can't wait to meet Lucy Goosey."

I left him deciding between white or orange cheese popcorn, grabbed a bag of potato sticks, and went to find Anna. I helped her check out and carried the bags to the truck where Neils was waiting for us, snoring loudly as he napped behind the wheel.

We made our way down Front Street. Just past the old bank building I could see two orange flags on top of a big sign near the water's edge that read *FINISH*.

"What's the sign for?" I asked Neils.

"That's the finish line for the Yukon River Quest, the longest paddle race in the world. They're expecting the first boat sometime tonight, I think."

"Sometime? Don't they know when the race is over?"

"It's a seven-hundred-and-fifteen-kilometre race. They left Whitehorse two days ago. The fastest teams take about forty-five hours to get here, and lots of racers don't make it at all. Tomorrow they'll be arriving all day."

A couple of porta-potties and a tent were also set up along the dike beside the river.

"Maybe Chris would like to come tomorrow and see for himself?" Anna said, lightly hitting Neils on the arm.

"Sure, sure."

I noticed Anna was always hinting to Neils to show me around Dawson more. She seemed pretty confident I'd be staying.

* * *

The next day Neils and I drove back into town and parked by the white gazebo on the river side of Front Street. People were standing on the trail that ran along the crest of the dike, looking at the water. The wind pulled at my sweater as we walked up to join them. The Yukon River current swept by Dawson quickly, as if the water was in a hurry to get to the Bering Sea. Over by the docks, three kayaks were on the beach and volunteers were helping a team in a voyageur-type canoe come ashore. The team was drenched in sweat and leaning on their paddles, which they balanced across the canoe.

"Who won?" I asked Neils.

"Ask Denise over there — the woman with the clipboard. She signs the teams in as they arrive."

Denise told me a kayak duo who called themselves Are We There Yet? came in Friday night. They had paddled for over forty-two hours to get here. I wondered where they went to the bathroom and how they ate while they were on the river, but I didn't dare ask.

I wanted so badly to let Dawson feel like home — to talk about the local festivals and races like I would be here to see them again next year. But part of me was afraid of settling in. What if Dad couldn't make a go of the mine? What if I was wrong and there really wasn't any gold on the claim and the nugget I had found in the cabin was from somewhere else? So, I held back a little, hoping it would protect me from getting hurt if it didn't work out here in the Yukon.

"Just the person I wanted to see!"

I looked around to see Vinnie striding over to me, his usual big grin pasted on his face.

"Hi, Vinnie. Survived Lucy, did you?"

Vinnie let out a belly laugh. "Love that goose! She's got a big personality. Came at me flapping and hissing, that great big beak ready to nip out a bit of skin, until I pulled out the jalapeno-cheese popcorn. She stopped dead in her tracks and started to *gleep, gleep, gleep* at me, gentle as a lamb. Gotta thank you for the tip, or I might be missing a nose or finger now."

"Glad to hear it works," I said, knowing at some point I'd probably be going back there with Neils.

"Gave me an idea too," Vinnie said. "Forget diet muffins . . . I'm going to sell gourmet popcorn! It's a low-calorie snack that even Dr. Bolton will approve of. I've already got some recipe ideas." Vinnie was almost quivering with excitement.

"But I have a favour to ask," he said. "Do you think your father would mind if I planted some vegetables and herbs in a little plot beside the cabin? I would happily share my crop. It's just everything in the General Store is so darn expensive, and you've got the land just sitting there . . ."

I thought it was a great idea. For my dad, I mean. He never was that reliable with feeding himself, or me for that matter. Having some fresh vegetables beside the cabin might remind him to eat.

"Sure. How about tomorrow? It's supposed to be sunny and warm."

"Yee-haw!" Vinnie said. "I'll go and see if the

Bonanza Market has any seed packets left. See you tomorrow."

I gave a wave as he bounded off, heading for the market on Second Avenue. A roar went up in the crowd and I scrambled back to the top of the dike. Upriver two canoes were racing to the finish line. Everyone on shore cheered them on. In the distance I could see someone standing on a paddleboard. I couldn't imagine paddling for days, all the way from Whitehorse. What a wild race.

"DON'T YOU EVER CHECK YOUR EMAIL?"

I jumped at the sound of someone yelling this in my ear. I spun around and was almost nose to nose with . . . Shard.

"What are you doing here?" I sputtered. I was ridiculously glad to see her. There are some things you can really only talk over with your best friend who knows what's happened to you. I had missed her straight talk. At times I felt over my head with how we were going to find the money to start mining, or how I was going to get the cabin ready for my dad, or how we were even going to find the gold, and I needed her view on things. Trouble was, she wasn't just down the hall anymore — she was thousands of kilometres away. Until now.

"I told you IN MY EMAIL," she said, loud enough that the people around us turned to stare, "that I was hitching a ride with Fiona."

"Fiona's here?" I asked, looking around. Even though her family lived in Dawson, I hadn't expected to see Fiona again so soon. Convincing her to help me get here had been tricky business. It was lucky she had some family stuff to take care of, otherwise there's no way she would have agreed to let me ride with her on the Ducati all the way to Dawson. I thought once she'd headed home again, it would be the last time I'd see her for a long time. After all, she had a business to run — and the Bull and Brambles bar did a roaring business.

"Yeah, she's over there smooching with Uncle Vinnie," Shard said, lifting her thumb over her shoulder. When Vinnie had offered to finish taking us and the broken-down Ducati to Dawson in his food truck, he and Fiona kinda hit it off and were always disappearing to be alone. Gave me hives. "Seems her mother broke her hip or something, and Fiona's sister was all, 'It's about time you take a turn running yourself ragged and getting lectured by mommy dearest.' And Fiona felt enough guilt that she said she'd come for a month."

"And she offered you a ride?" I asked, suspiciously. Fiona was not known for her warmth or consideration. You have to be tough to bounce clients who've had enough to drink.

"Nah, my mom promised her some gas money

if she'd take me. I'm supposed to check up on Uncle Vinnie. My mom says her little brother is like a firecracker in a welding shop — she never knows when he'll go off. Says he's been up here too long without anyone checking up on him."

"Did Vinnie know you were coming? He never said anything to me."

"Yes, because HE CHECKS HIS EMAIL."

I guess Vinnie thought I already knew and was too excited about his new gourmet popcorn venture to say anything.

The crowd on the dike roared as the paddleboarder crossed the finish line.

"So, where are you staying?"

"With Uncle Vinnie. He's renting an apartment in some hideous salmon-coloured fourplex on Sixth Avenue here in Dawson."

That was news to me, but then living forty-five minutes away, I didn't come into town much. "Vinnie's coming out to the claim tomorrow to plant a garden. Are you coming with him?"

"I guess so. I'll ask him, if he ever gets his lips unlocked long enough to answer me." We both shuddered.

Neils waved me over, signalling it was time to leave. "See you tomorrow, then," I said.

Shard gave a salute and went to find Vinnie.

I felt better than I had in a long time.

CHAPTER 5

MISSING TREASURE

"Why are there so many rocks?" Shard asked, throwing a baseball-sized one into the bush.

"Neils said that finding layers of rocks and pebbles means this section has already been mined and that's where we should garden," I said.

"That's because Neils isn't the one having to plant in this gravel pit," she grumbled.

I had to agree. Every time my shovel went in, it scraped and banged against rocks.

"Look what Mrs. Lockhart gave me," Vinnie said, beaming. "Cuttings from her herb garden — sage, lavender, oregano and parsley. She won an award last year for her yard, you know."

"What award?" Shard asked.

"Most improved, I think," Vinnie answered. "And I went to the market, and although there weren't very many left, I found a few packets of seeds — so I got carrot, turnip, basil, onion and a few garlic bulbs. And they were about to throw out some rather wilted veggie seedlings, so they gave me these tomato and pepper plants for free! I can't wait to start concocting delicious flavour combinations."

I didn't know what to say to him. Turnip? Parsley? Peppers? Who would buy popcorn with those hideous flavours? I didn't think even Lucy Goosey, as Vinnie called her, would eat turnip popcorn. But my dad wouldn't turn his nose up at some turnip and carrot mash. Mom used to make that at Thanksgiving. I felt the pang of missing her, but I shook it off. Mom had taken off on me and my dad almost two years ago. Even when I dared ask Dad about her, I never got the impression she was coming back. It didn't do any good to wish for things you couldn't have.

I positioned the shovel for another row and put my foot on the edge to help it go into the hard ground. I pushed down and heard a scraping sound.

"What was that?" Shard asked.

"I don't know, but it wasn't a rock. It sounded like metal. Help me dig around the spot so we can pull up whatever it is."

Shard and I carefully dug down.

"I see it!" I said, reaching into the hole. There

was a bent handle on top of a rusty canister. I pulled on it and the soil loosened its grip.

"I've seen one of those before," Vinnie said, loping back over to us. "That's a miner's lamp."

I turned it around and saw a disc in the middle with a small nozzle where the flame must have come out. It was in pretty good shape considering it must have been under the ground for years — there was just a small crack near the rim of the glass.

"This looks original," Vinnie said, taking it from me and having a close look. "I saw some in the Trading Post and this is the same. Definitely early 1900s."

He handed it back to me. "I think it was your granddad's."

I smiled as I took it. There was no way of knowing for sure who had lost it, of course. But either way, it was our claim now so it belonged to us. I walked over and set it on the ground just outside the cabin door so we wouldn't damage it any more.

Once the ground was ready, Vinnie provided lunch in the form of ham-and-cheese muffins. We sat in the shade of some pine trees and used a fallen tree as a bench.

"So, do you think you might stay longer than a month?" I asked Shard.

Shard cast a glance at her uncle. "Depends on a few things. One of them being if Fiona stays longer than she planned, since she *is* my ride back. She said as soon as her mom is able to look after herself, or her sister takes over, she'd be heading back to our old stomping grounds in the city. But you never know — things could get delayed."

You know what was weird? I got this pang when I thought of Shard leaving again. It's the same one I get when anyone leaves: my dad being hauled off to jail; my mom going away and not coming back. I did my best to hang on to people around me, but it didn't always work. I hadn't made a lot of friends living way out of town at Neils's place and ones like Shard didn't come along every day.

We munched our lunch muffins and washed them down with some lemonade. There were double chocolate muffins for dessert.

"Ew," Shard said, pointing at the end of our tree bench as she chewed. "What is that?"

I looked over to see a big bulbous growth on the trunk. It was huge and bumpy. It looked like the tree had swallowed a watermelon that got stuck partway down.

I had no idea what it was, but then everything was so odd here, why not the trees too? I bet my dad would know. I'd have to remember to ask.

We finished our picnic lunch, then got down to the work of planting the cuttings, plants, bulbs and seeds. I worked on making rows for the seeds. Shard was planting the garlic bulbs.

"Are there shafts around here?" Shard asked.

"I don't think so. Why?"

"Because I've hit wood," she said.

I ran over to see. We made the hole bigger with our trowels. It wasn't a beam Shard had hit, but a small wooden box with the initials *WD* carved into the lid. That just had to stand for my granddad, Wally Dearing. There was a tiny metal clasp on one side, and when I flipped it open, I could see a small device inside. Lifting it out made it obvious it was a little set of scales.

"It must be for measuring gold," I said. I went over to the cabin door, picked up the lamp, and went inside. I carefully tucked the lamp and the scales up in the rafters near where I had found the toe and the nugget. My fingers tingled with excitement from touching things that were my granddad's, but deep down there was a pinprick of worry that they had something to do with the dredge robbery and that's why they were buried in the ground.

We finished up by filling buckets from the

creek and giving the plants and seeds their first watering. That's when it hit me . . . there was no running water at the cabin. Dad and I were going to have to rough it.

"Well, we might not have found gold today, but there certainly were treasures," Vinnie said. "This garden is already paying off!"

I realized I hadn't had the chance to tell Shard about the nugget, which was now safely stashed away in my sock drawer. I wanted to do it in private because although Vinnie was a great guy, I wasn't sure he could keep news like that to himself, and I didn't need everyone in town knowing about it.

I just hoped a few artifacts and one small nugget weren't the only treasures we would find on the claim.

CHAPTER 6

UP IN SMOKE

Bullet yipped in excitement for his breakfast. I gave him a pat on the head before using the enormous ladle to slop some sled dog stew into his bowl. The other dogs barked excitedly, impatient for their own helping. I watched as Bullet dove into his food with the same enthusiasm I used for Anna's chicken pot pie. It was a great feeling to be greeted so eagerly as I made my way from doghouse to doghouse with the bucket.

"So, you're making friends with my pals, heh?" Neils said, as I finished and handed him the empty bucket. "How would you like to help me work them this summer?"

"Really? I can take them out for a run?"

"Well, not alone. We'll start out going together, but once I see you have good control, it would free me up a bit. If they don't get some training this summer, we won't be ready for the Yukon Quest in February."

"Didn't we just watch the end of that race?"

"No, that was the Yukon *River* Quest. That's a paddling race. The Yukon Quest is a sled dog race."

"Did they run out of names for things?" I asked.

"Ha ha ha." Neils laughed heartily, as if I'd said the funniest thing.

But I was being serious. I hadn't gotten used to Dawson City yet — it was a strange place. There were no paved roads, or sidewalks, or traffic lights. There wasn't even a bridge over the river to get to West Dawson. You had to take this tiny ferry that sailed sideways to fight the Yukon River current. The tallest buildings in town were only three storeys high, and most of them were painted weird, bright colours. I wondered if that was so you could see them in the winter when everything was white with snow.

Still, I was excited at the prospect of running the dogs. Wouldn't it feel great to have the wind in your face as you whizzed along?

"Won't the stones wreck the sled runners?" I asked.

Neils broke out in laughter again. "We use a wagon with wheels in the summer, Chris."

I flushed. Sure, now I know it sounded like a dumb question, but how was I supposed to know what they did in this place where you can't even tell what time it is in the summer because it's sunny day and night.

After we had our own breakfast, Neils showed me how to harness the dogs and hook them to the gangline. Bullet was lead dog and looked back at us as we took our positions on the wagon along the dirt lane leading away from the house. One word from Neils and we were off — the dogs were strong and fast! We zipped along beside Cottonwood Creek until we crossed at one spot that was shallow and sandy, the water splashing up all around us. Then we started back along the other side. Neils explained what commands to give the dogs. He let me give some of them, but the dogs weren't sure if they should do as I said or not.

"Say it like you mean it," Neils instructed.

"Haw," I said, leaning to the left to bank the corner.

"Better," Neils said.

We raced along an overgrown path beside the creek. In the valley up ahead was the border of my granddad's claim. Somewhere at the far end from where we were, hidden among the trees, was the rundown cabin I still hadn't fixed up.

I was scanning the area, wondering if I could see it, when I noticed a thin line of smoke rising from the woods.

"Neils! I think the cabin is on fire!" I shouted.

Neils looked up quickly, and I could see his face darken. "I sure hope you're wrong," he said.

Neils took over with the team and hurried them on in the direction of the cabin. The path got narrower and narrower and low branches threatened to clothesline us. It was obvious it hadn't been used in years. My heart was thudding in my chest. If the cabin burned down, where would my dad stay? An old, decrepit wooden structure was better than a pile of ashes.

We couldn't get right up to the cabin because the path faded away and trees and saplings blocked our route. As soon as the sled slowed down, I hopped off and sprinted straight for the cabin.

"Chris! It's not safe! Come back!" Neils called.

I kept running — I had to do something to stop the fire. I raced through the brush, thorny stalks scratching my arms and face as I barrelled toward the small clearing where the log structure stood. Smoke was billowing out the chimney. I pushed the door open and it rocked on its hinges. In that split second, everything changed.

CHAPTER 7

SO CLOSE AND YET SO FAR

"Dad!"

My father stood up and smiled. I ran into his arms, out of breath.

"Chris!" he said, pulling me into a big hug. Then he pushed me back a bit and looked me up and down. "You look good, like you've put on a bit of weight. And maybe taller too." He tousled my hair.

I wanted to say the same to him, but the truth was he looked terrible. His shirt hung off his bony shoulders, and he had a scruffy beard that stood out on his pale face. But I figured a few weeks up here with some decent food, fresh air and hard work would have him back to the way he was when I last saw him a month ago. Maybe even the way he was before Mom left.

"How did you know I was here?" he asked.

"I saw the smoke from the chimney. I thought

the whole cabin was on fire," I panted.

"Well, if I don't get this fireplace cleaned out, you might be right."

"I'll help," I said.

The light inside dimmed as Neils blocked the doorway.

My dad straightened his shoulders, and the two of them stared at each other. I don't know how much Mrs. CPS had actually told Neils and Anna about my dad and how he struggled to look after me. Don't get me wrong, I didn't mind trying to hide the rent money so Dad wouldn't be tempted to drink it away, and I never complained about having nothing but pickles and crackers for supper more often than not. I hoped that stuff was confidential and that Mrs. Olsen hadn't said anything. I didn't want them thinking bad about my dad. My dad walked over to Neils. I held my breath, worried for a second about what he was going to do, but he stuck out his hand and Neils shook it.

"You must be Neils," he said.

Neils nodded. "It's nice to finally meet you, Francis, is it?"

"Call me Frank." They stopped shaking hands.

Neils turned to me, "Come on, Chris. We need to be going."

I looked from Neils to my dad and back again.

I couldn't believe Neils was making me leave. "But he just got here! And he needs my help."

"Your dad can take care of himself. Besides, we have to get the dogs back."

"But . . ."

"He's right, Chris. I'm fine here. And I've got a lot to do. You run along. I'll see you soon." Dad didn't seem to have any fight left in him.

I followed Neils out in a bit of a daze. "Why couldn't I stay?" I asked, a swell of anger rising up.

Neils untied the wagon from a tree. The dogs sprang to their feet. "It's the rules."

"What rules?"

Neils sighed. "It's going to take a bit of time before you can go back to your dad. He has to prove to Mrs. Olsen and Child Protective Services that he can take care of you."

"But he's my *dad*!"

"I know it's hard to understand, but give it a bit of time, and as long as everything goes well, you'll be with your dad again real soon."

I was glad I was facing forward on the wagon so Neils couldn't see that I was almost crying. I thought my dad would come and we'd be back together like always. And I knew what *"as long as everything goes well"* meant: as long as my dad stayed sober. I hated the idea of someone else deciding whether or not I could be with him.

Once we were back and I helped unharness the dogs, I trudged to the house. The best I could manage was to pick at my lunch, even though I loved fish tacos. I saw Neils and Anna exchange glances, but I was glad they didn't say anything to me. I didn't feel like talking. Then a thought came to me: Our claim wasn't that far away. Who was to stop me from just heading over there this afternoon? I would tell Neils that I was going to clean out the dog yard or something. But almost as if he guessed what I was thinking, Neils asked me to come along to his claim after lunch to wash and sort some of the items they had dug up while mining.

It was torture to know that my dad was so close and I wasn't with him.

* * *

Neils and I bumped along the road, kicking up clouds of dust behind us. Alone in the truck was usually a good time to talk to Neils. I wanted to ask about my dad and how long Neils thought it would take for me to go back to live with him, but I could sense Neils didn't want to talk about it. So, I decided to find out about something else that was bugging me.

"Neils?" I said.

"Hmmhuh?"

"What happened with my granddad at Dredge Number Two?"

Neils never took his eyes off the road. "Some things are better left in the past."

I felt frustration bubbling up, but I didn't push. I know when someone isn't going to tell you anything. That's the way it was with my dad whenever I asked about my mom.

We rode in silence the rest of the way. At the claim Neils had to help Dave pull the mats from the sluice for a cleanup, so Leo showed me the plastic bin where they dumped any artifacts they found while mining. Everything was covered with so much mud it was hard to see what was there.

"Found some old flasks and tools in the new cut the last few days," Leo said. "Never know if it's junk or not until we clean them up. Glad you're here to help."

Leo and I used stiff brushes to get dried mud off the different items. We didn't want to damage anything before we knew if it was valuable. While we worked, I wondered about the lamp and gold scales I found on Granddad's claim.

"Hey, Leo? You said that my granddad was accused of robbery."

Leo looked up at me and gulped.

"What did they say he stole?" I asked.

Leo looked around nervously.

"I'm not sure I should . . ."

"Come on, Leo. I'm his grandson. I have a right to know."

Leo gave one more glance around, as if he was worried someone would hear. "Gold. They say he stole a bag of gold dust and nuggets from the gold room on the dredge."

My heart sank. All I could think of was the nugget that had been hidden in the cabin. "A lot of gold or just a nugget or two?"

Leo snorted. "Any gold is a serious crime. He practically had a bounty on his head. They couldn't find him for three days. When they did, he was bold enough to have the gold on him, walking into town to sell it to a gold buyer." Leo shook his head. "Claimed it wasn't stolen. Said he hadn't been in hiding, he was out prospecting. Said he mined the gold on his claim. Of course, no one believed him. Everyone knew that claim was worthless."

"How come you know so much about this? It must have happened a long time ago." Deep down I was hoping this was just a story that grew every time someone told it. Or maybe it was all Leo's imagination.

"Everyone remembers Wally's gold. Was the talk of Dawson for years. My wife, Margie, works at the archives during the summer. When she heard Neils was taking in a Dearing, she told me it reminded her that they have a huge file on the whole episode."

Nope. Not imagined. Of course a bad story about the Dearings had to be true. But a small part of me hoped it was exaggerated in some way.

"Where are the archives?" I asked.

Leo didn't answer for a moment. "You want to know it all, don't you?"

I nodded.

"Well, I'll ask Margie if she can help you out."

"Thanks, Leo," I said, meaning it. Knowing, even if it was bad, was always better than not knowing.

Leo went off to help with the gold cleanup, so I had some time to think while I scraped mud. If I was being honest, I was kind of mad at my dad. I mean, I was so happy he was here and I just wanted to be with him, but he told me to go off with Neils like he didn't need me. I wished sometimes he would fight for me as hard as I fought for him.

"So, what have we got?" Neils asked, coming over.

I pushed all those thoughts back in the corners of my mind for later. I held up some rusty metal trays and what looked like parts of tools.

"Ah, pouring trays. And this is an axe head,"

Neils said, turning the triangular metal piece in his hand. "Very nice. Let's put them in my museum."

"You have a museum?"

Neils laughed. "Well, that's what we call it. It's just a collection I store in this old cabin. I put most of the stuff we find in there, except anything worth a bit of money. Ian at the Trading Post sells those for me."

We carried over the metal objects, and Neils shoved the door open with his shoulder. Kettles, cans and pots were piled on tables and shelves. Bigger items like axes and shovels were on the floor. The walls were covered with signs and pictures. One huge map was pinned up and showed all the mountains, valleys, rivers, creeks and roads from 1851. I found my granddad's claim by following Cottonwood Creek with my finger from where it started up by Forty Mile, all the way down to where it crossed the road heading out of Dawson and cut right through the middle of Claim 427. That's what our claim was labelled. I knew it was the right one because Neils had highlighted his original claim beside it.

As I stepped forward for a closer look, I stubbed my toe on a piece of curved beige wood that was leaning against a cabinet. It was almost as long as I was tall.

"What's that?" I asked.

"Woolly mammoth tusk. It broke in half, here, see? It was about twice as long as this in real life."

The mammoth it came from must have been massive! Bigger than any animal I had ever seen. I touched the tusk. Its surface was smooth, like a polished piece of wood.

BANG! We both straightened up at the sound.

"Oh no. Not the D10 again," Neils said. "If we lose much more time this season, I won't even be able to cover my fuel costs."

We ran out of the log cabin. All looked calm over where the sluice was. And the D10 was working away. No, the sound was coming from behind us and the noise was getting louder and louder. In between the bangs was a high squeal. It was almost like a pig that had eaten too many beans.

When we turned around, we saw a contraption that was once a motorbike, I think. Every part seemed to be a different colour, and none of it looked like it belonged on the same machine. It could only be Vinnie's. The Frankenbike coasted to a stop. It was only then that I noticed Shard sitting behind Vinnie.

"What do you think of my ride?" Vinnie asked us, taking off his helmet, beaming.

Neils and I groped for words.

"Well, you won't be sneaking up on us," Neils said, finally. "And the noise will probably keep the bears away." Neils raised his eyebrows at me.

"Yeah, and it'll be handy on the narrow roads," I added. "Easy to swerve around potholes."

Shard took off her helmet and rolled her eyes. "It's a monster. My ears are still ringing from the engine, and my teeth were almost knocked out of my head going over ruts in the road. Doesn't this thing have shock absorbers?"

Vinnie looked at his bike with confusion. "Not sure. But Fiona said she was going to take a look at it tomorrow."

"I hope she doesn't bring a blowtorch," Shard said. "Because she's gonna take one look at this thing and want to melt it into a ball of iron, then throw it to the ravens at the town dump."

I saw Neils trying not to laugh because Vinnie looked so proud of his wheels.

"So, what can I do for you?" Neils asked.

"Well, I'm adding gourmet popcorn to my menu and I want to make kettle corn. Gord suggested I ask if you have an old iron kettle in what he called your 'museum,'" Vinnie said.

Neils rubbed his chin. "You know, I just might have something that will work." The two of them headed back into the log cabin.

"You look like you've just run over a squirrel or something," Shard told me.

"My dad's here," I blurted out.

"He is? Where?" Shard looked around as if he was hiding in the bushes.

"At the cabin on our claim."

"Well, that's good. Looks like he got off easy."

"I guess." Was going to jail, even for a few weeks, easy? "I just thought when he got up here, we'd be together again. But Neils pulled me away and my dad just let him. Something about it being the rules." My voice cracked a little.

"Well, yeah," Shard said. "You don't get to just go back like nothing happened. There's this whole process."

I looked down at the gravel. "What process?"

"I don't know specifics, but Darrin Pomeroy had to go to some centre once a week to meet with his mother in a room with two-way mirrors."

"How long did that last?" I asked, my stomach dropping.

"Dunno. He moved away before I found out."

"Oh." Why was it every time I thought things were getting sorted out, it all went screwy again? Dad was here but I couldn't be with him. He was on the claim but I didn't know how we were going to get any equipment. The mining season was underway but we still had nothing.

CHAPTER 8

WHAT'S IN A NAME?

Neils kept me pretty busy over the next few days. All of a sudden he seemed to need a lot of help at his claim — sorting artifacts, helping with the gold cleanup, washing mud off rubber boots, fetching and carrying.

This morning I was determined to see my dad. I had finished giving the dogs their breakfast stew and was about to scurry down the lane to head to our claim when I heard an engine getting closer. Around the bend came Vinnie and Shard on a motorbike that looked the same as the Frankenbike but didn't sound it.

"Wow, that sounds better," I said, as Vinnie came to a stop and Shard hopped off. "Almost didn't think it was the same bike."

"Fiona made a few adjustments," Vinnie said, removing his helmet to reveal his cheeks turning pink.

"Few adjustments?" Shard said, snorting. "She practically rebuilt the entire engine." Shard looked at me. "Called it a monstrosity and said it was going to give her nightmares. Ever see that cartoon of the Tasmanian Devil? That's what she looked like while working on it."

I smiled. I could totally see it. "What are you doing here?" I asked her.

"We're off to water the garden again. Just thought we'd stop in and say hi."

"What do you mean, 'again'?"

"The garden isn't going to grow without water," Shard said. "We're out there every other day watering and weeding till we almost drop."

"So, *you* can see my dad, but I can't?!"

For the first time ever, Shard seemed to have nothing to say.

"I'm going over there right now," I said. "Vinnie, will you give me a ride?"

Vinnie smiled widely. "Sure thing. Hop on. Shard, lend him your helmet and I'll be back for you in a minute."

Before Shard could hand it over, Anna came out of the house.

"Well, hi, Vinnie, Shard. That bike was so quiet, I didn't even hear you come down the lane."

"Hello, Anna," Vinnie said. "I'm just going to give Chris here a lift over to the Dearing claim, and I brought you a sample of my newest product to try — lavender and honey popcorn. I call it Luscious Lavender."

He pulled a small paper bag out of the pocket of his jacket and handed it to her. Anna took a wary sniff and looked up at Vinnie with a big smile.

"That's so, so inventive! I'm really looking forward to trying it."

Vinnie's face fell. It was plain he wanted her to try his concoction right away.

"I want to enjoy it with my tea. I think it will go wonderfully with Earl Grey."

That seemed to satisfy him.

"And I'm afraid I need Chris to come into town with me," she added.

I swivelled my head to stare at her. Come into town? No one had mentioned a trip into town to me. I felt like a puppet being jerked around by everyone.

"Righto," Vinnie said, snapping his helmet on and motioning for Shard to climb aboard.

"I'll, uh, see you around," Shard said.

"Say hi to my dad for me," I said, angrily following Anna to her small red car. We drove into town, bumping over the gravel roads. Anna kept up a chatter about the recent bear sightings and peonies that belonged to someone named

Mrs. Pomfrey, but I didn't answer. I didn't ask her where we were going, because if it wasn't to the claim to see my dad, I didn't care. We pulled into the Northern Lights Support Services parking lot. Now I *did* care. What was going on?

"What are we doing here?" I asked Anna, not even unbuckling my seat belt.

"An information session. Come on."

There's one thing about Anna — she might look sweet and mild, but she has a spine of iron. She got out of the car and started walking. She gave me one glance back, raising her eyebrows. I knew when I was beat — I got out of the car.

We went in and were directed to room four. Anna opened the door briskly. I dragged my feet. Then I froze at the sound of a voice I dreaded.

"Good morning, Mrs. Amundson, Chris." It was Mrs. Olsen. She rose from her chair and held out a hand to Anna, who shook it.

I said nothing. I just stared her down. From across the room, Anna gave me a bit of a look that said *be polite*.

"Morning," I mumbled.

"Neils and I thought it would be good if Mrs. Olsen cleared up some things about your father," Anna said.

I plunked down on a pre-formed plastic chair and just glared.

Mrs. Olsen cleared her throat. "So, Chris, this part of the process . . ."

"Why can't I see my dad?" I blurted out. "Everyone is keeping me away from him. He served his time and he needs my help on the claim."

"You can't just go back like nothing happened," she said. "This will take time."

"Why?"

"Because we have to make sure you are going to be taken care of."

"He's my *dad*."

"Yes, but we want to make sure you won't end up in the same situation in a couple of months. Your dad needs a bit of time to get back on his feet. The cabin isn't winterized. There is no sanitary water supply, no bathroom, no separate sleeping quarters for you, no power. How does your dad plan to survive the winter there? How would you get to school? These things have to be arranged."

"So, I can't see him until then?" My voice cracked on that, giving away how close to tears I was.

"Of course you can. But we'll start with supervised visits for a few hours. If all goes well, you can have some unsupervised visits and even stay over. If he makes the improvements to the cabin, we can talk about a timeline for you living with him again."

I didn't answer. I could hear that it was no use arguing — the system was against me.

"When can I see him?" I asked.

"Well, seeing as I'm in town now, why don't we say this afternoon?"

Anna nodded. I folded my arms. Mrs. Olsen kept talking but I tuned it all out. I wasn't interested in their "process."

Anna and I stopped in at the General Store for some groceries before we headed back. I wondered if my dad had enough food, or whether he was living on dill pickles and crackers again. I rounded the narrow corner by the bread display and bumped into another shopper, almost knocking a frozen pizza out of her hands.

"Well, if it isn't Dirk Stark," she said.

I looked up in surprise. I hadn't heard that name since I left our apartment, what felt like years ago. I had planned on legally changing my name to Dirk Stark when I turned eighteen in order to not be lumped in with all the other loser Dearings. And now with a robber grandfather and an ex-con father, it was probably still a good idea. But I didn't think Fiona would have remembered that.

"Just the person I was hoping to run into," Fiona said. "Do you remember that cheese my mother likes? You know, the one you picked up for me before we came up here?"

It was a sad fact that I did remember. That whole shopping trip was a humiliating nightmare. I was just glad Fiona wasn't asking me what size pantyhose her mother wore — because I knew that too.

"Gorgonzola. Spicy."

"Oh, right. Thanks. Mom just muttered something about wanting cheese when I said I was coming into town. And I had better get the right kind or I'm going to hear about it."

It made me giggle to think of biker Fiona still being told what to do by her mother.

"I'm sorry to hear about your mother's hip," I said. "I hope she's getting better."

Fiona rolled her eyes. "Who can tell? In between all the complaining about my cooking, she hasn't really said."

Anna came around the corner, her shopping cart half full. Fiona turned around and I could see her stiffen. "Anna," she said.

"Fiona."

I looked from one to the other. There was enough tension between them to snap a wire.

"Come on, Chris. We need to get home for lunch and then we have that appointment," Anna said.

"I guess I'll see you around," I said to Fiona.

The only time Anna said anything on the drive back was when she cursed at the tourists meandering every which way across the roads in town.

Back at the house, I grabbed some kielbasa sausage and a few crackers for lunch, ignoring Anna's insistence that I eat "a decent meal." I headed out to sit with Bullet and share a bit of the sausage with him. He showed his appreciation by licking my ear. I stayed out with the dogs, getting them fresh water and cleaning out their food bowls, until I heard a car pull up in the driveway. I hurried back. I hated that Mrs. Olsen had to come with me, but I was going to see my dad!

CHAPTER 9

I DON'T HAVE A CLUE

Mrs. Olsen's car had barely rolled to a stop on the Dearing claim when I opened the door and jumped out. I ran to the cabin, and the first thing I noticed was that the hinges had been fixed and the door swung open easily. Inside, well, I wouldn't say it was luxury living, or even comfortable living, but Dad had fixed the shelves and the bed, there was a table and chair in the corner, and the floor had been swept . . . or maybe just shovelled, but still, he was making an effort. Looking up, I could just see the corner of the wooden box with the gold scales inside, and a glint of the light on the glass of the lamp beside it. I realized I still hadn't told Dad about the artifacts. I'd have to remember to tell him when we were alone.

Mrs. Olsen took it all in as she stood in the doorway. "Good day, Mr. Dearing. How is the water situation?" she asked, getting right down to business.

"Got a pump coming tomorrow," Dad said, getting up from the chair and rubbing a hand across his scraggly beard.

"Can you show me around the claim?" I asked my dad. Actually, I just wanted to get out of earshot of Mrs. Olsen so I could ask him some things that were bugging me.

"Sure." Dad gave a nod to Mrs. Olsen, who followed us out, then trailed behind as we strode along a path that led behind the cabin. There was an old shed back there that I had never noticed.

"What's that?"

"Looks like the guys who swindled your granddad out of the claim built themselves a bathhouse for when they were working out here. There even seemed to be running water from the well they dug on the other side of the cabin. No roughing it for them," he said. "The well pump's shot though, so I have to get a new one."

I stepped through the open doorway and stopped. The sink was rusted through and the toilet had a big crack down one side. Thank goodness the lid was down, since there was no way I wanted to look in there. The roof of the bathhouse was still on but it had a few holes in it, and some of the frame had rotted away so the whole building was leaning to the left.

We went back outside and continued through the bush to a bit of a clearing.

"Are you going to start mining soon?" I asked.

Dad stopped in the clearing. "Sure am. Just have to get some equipment first."

"How will you afford that? You know, Neils said he could probably get you—"

"I don't need Neils's help," Dad said, cutting me off.

"He just wants to . . ."

"I've got something in the works."

I went quiet. It was obvious that no matter how many connections Neils had, my dad wasn't going to use them.

"Do you remember you said Granddad told you where the pay streak was when he was on his deathbed?" I said, changing the subject.

"Yup."

"Well, what did he say?"

My dad looked to see that Mrs. Olsen was still far enough away. "He told me that 'the gold is as good as in the bank.'"

As good as in the bank? That was the message? It just sounded like Granddad was telling him where he kept his money.

"I don't get it. How is that a clue? It's just a saying, isn't it?"

"It would be, except your granddad didn't believe in banks. Wouldn't keep so much as a shin plaster in one."

"Shin plaster?"

"A twenty-five-cent paper note."

"Quarters were made of paper?"

"Yeah, and so worthless that people used them as bandages."

"Oh. I still don't get the clue, though."

"The gold is along the banks of Cottonwood Creek," he whispered.

We walked in silence for a while.

"*That's* what you think he meant?" I wasn't convinced. I expected Granddad's deathbed clue to be something more concrete, like: *Find the rock that looks like a turtle, take ten paces south and start digging*. "How can you be sure you're right?"

"He was my dad. I knew him better than anyone. We mined together for years — until I left, that is."

"Why *did* you leave?"

"I told you, to find work. He wasn't mining any gold and I was tired of being hungry." He shrugged.

"So, he never got another claim?"

"Oh, he bought and sold two or three after he lost this one, but they were all worthless."

"So, why didn't you come back to help him?" I knew I'd do anything to help my dad.

Dad put his hands in his jean pockets. "We had an argument. We stopped talking."

"Over what?"

"See where the creek bends just over there on the edge of our claim?" he said. "That's where I'm going to start mining. Gold collects where water slows down, and the water has to slow to go around the corner."

It was obvious he wasn't going to answer the question.

"When are you going to start?" The sooner he got going, the sooner I would get to move in.

"Any day now. Just have to get my gear."

I nodded. We walked some more, talking about his plans for where the sluice would go, the tailings pile and the cut. What we didn't talk about was my dad's time in jail, his drinking, money or my mom. All the important topics. I wanted to know if he had stopped hanging out in bars, if we could afford mining equipment, and most of all, if he had heard from Mom. But I'm sure we'd have some quiet time to talk about those things when I was with him again.

"Chris!" Mrs. Olsen called from where she was standing under a pine. "Time's up. We need to be going."

I looked up at my dad. Would he insist we have a few more minutes?

"He's coming," he said, herding us back toward the cabin.

Fight for me! I screamed silently inside my head.

I watched him go into the log structure as I climbed into Mrs. Olsen's car for the short trip to Neils's house. We rode in silence. When we got into Neils's driveway a few minutes later, he met us outside.

"When can I see my dad again?" I asked Mrs. Olsen, as I got out of the car.

"Well, I'm heading back to Whitehorse this afternoon. I'll try and come next week."

"Next week!? I'm not waiting that long."

"I can't come back before then. It's a six-hour drive and I do have other clients."

Neils looked at me. "That's not gonna fly," he said to her. "A boy needs his dad."

"Well, that's the best I can do."

"Then I'll supervise the visits," Neils said.

"That's not protocol," Mrs. Olsen said, but I could see her grimacing. She knew what she was up against with Neils.

"Then gas up your car, because you'll be spending a lot of time driving to and from Dawson," he said.

I looked at him, unused to the feeling of someone sticking up for me.

Mrs. Olsen put her head down on the steering wheel and sighed.

"Let me see if I can clear it, okay?" she said. "But no visits until I work this out."

"So long as you call before Thursday, 'cause that's when I have time to take him over there."

"That's in three days!"

"Yup," Neils said, walking away.

I followed Neils to the house, glad that he was on my side.

CHAPTER 10

LET'S MAKE A DEAL

"Want to come along?" Neils asked me the next morning as I shovelled down a bowl of granola. Anna had made it herself and it was tasty but just never seemed to fill me up.

"Sure! Where we going?"

"Flash Gordon's. Grizzly bars need replacing."

"Grizzly bears?"

"No, bars. They keep the biggest rocks out of the sluice so they can't wreck the belts."

"Oh," I said, never quite sure if Neils was teasing me or not. "Actually, I wouldn't mind poking around for a few things myself."

"Good. We'll leave in ten minutes." He got up and went outside.

I finished my bowl and took it to the sink.

"Hey, Anna," I said, rinsing out the milk. "Do you have any popcorn?"

"Planning on bribing Lucy?" she asked.

Sometimes I wondered if Anna was psychic.

"Something like that."

"Smart move. I keep telling Neils he should take some, but he flares up and yells that he isn't afraid of a guard goose. And you're in luck — I think I still have some of that purple lavender popcorn Vinnie gave me to try." She flushed pink. "I forgot to have it with my tea."

"That'd be great. She's one scary goose."

Anna dug out the paper bag from the cupboard and handed it over. I met Neils by the pickup truck and climbed in.

"So, what're you looking for this morning?" Neils asked me, as we roared down the lane.

"Well, I can't move in with my dad until he's got a sanitary bathroom for us. When he showed me the old bathhouse, the sink and toilet were no good anymore, so I wondered if maybe there's something in the junkyard we could use."

"I'm sure your dad's already thought of that. There's lots of fixtures there, and I'm sure Gord will make your dad a good deal."

I didn't bother correcting Neils, but I knew my dad needed me to help him. Now, how to pay for it — that was the part I hadn't figured out yet. But I would worry about that later. Maybe Dad had a bit of cash stashed away.

It had rained overnight and the road was

nothing but slick mud. I held my breath as we slid around some of the corners. I think mud is worse than dust on the roads. We finally turned down the lane to the junkyard and I saw the dredge up ahead. I realized that my granddad must have travelled on this very road to go to work. It made shivers go up and down my spine.

When we got to the yard, Neils turned the engine off, slowly opened the door, and carefully stepped out. I took my paper bag and did the same. All was quiet. We both breathed and began walking toward the dredge.

"I'm gonna go find Gord and ask him . . ." Neils started.

The rest of the sentence was lost in the noise of an ear-splitting screech. Lucy suddenly appeared from behind the hubcap tower, spread her wings, and ran straight at us, hissing.

"Ahhhhh!" Neils yelled, turning and running back to the truck.

Lucy turned her black-dot eyes on me. In a panic, I reached into the paper bag in my pocket and wildly threw a handful of popcorn at her. She skidded to a stop and stared at the slightly purple puffs on the ground.

Gleep, gleep, she said, snatching two in one swoop of her beak. She eyed me again. She shook her head slightly as if trying to figure out what odd flavour combination this was. I threw another handful. She flapped her wings and bobbed her head, then pecked at her treat some more.

"Nice goosey," I said, stepping sideways around her. "Nice Lucy." I threw some more near her for good measure and headed for the dredge. Lucy was completely preoccupied with snatching up the purple popcorn. Neils cautiously got back out of the truck and gave her a wide berth as he scooted past, then practically ran to the dredge while looking over his shoulder.

"Maniac," he said, glancing back at her. She raised her head and looked at him like she knew he was talking about her. She gave a small hiss and went back to her popcorn.

"Do you want some popcorn in your pocket, just in case?" I asked.

"I'm not giving in to her threats," he muttered, going into the dredge.

Stepping inside was like entering the belly of a mechanical whale. Massive wooden spools were lined up in front of us, and Neils told me they used to hold thick wire cables. Behind them and to the left the space opened up into a huge cavern where more massive machines used to stand.

"Hello?" a voice called from above us.

"Hello, Gord. It's Neils and Chris," Neils called back.

"Be right down." In a moment Gordon came down a narrow wooden staircase next to the door, his running shoes barely making a squeak. His eyes had dark circles and his shoulders drooped.

"You okay?" Neils asked him.

"Didn't get much sleep last night with the storm."

"What storm? It just rained."

Gordon wagged his finger. "Where there's rain clouds, there's chance of an electrical storm."

"Right, sorry. Hope we're not interrupting," Neils said.

"Not at all. I was just enjoying a Golden Nugget muffin. Vinnie's a genius."

"Um, yeah."

"He might still have some in his backpack, if you hurry," Gordon said.

"He's here?" I asked.

"Yeah, he and his niece are around back looking for parts for his food truck."

"I'm going to go say hi," I told Neils.

He nodded. "Just watch out for . . . for wild animals," Neils said, not mentioning Lucy by name.

I patted my pocket where the popcorn was. "I'll be careful."

I went back outside and around to the right.

It was like a maze through the piles of scrap.

"Does that even work?"

It was Shard's voice. I followed the sound of it around a heap of rusty and battered oil drums. She and Vinnie were standing near an old wooden door that was laid across two of the oil drums to make a kind of table. On it were motors of all sizes. The larger ones were sitting on the ground under the makeshift table.

"Hi, guys," I said. "What are you up to?"

"Hiya, Chris!" Vinnie answered. "Well, now that I have some popcorn recipes tried out, I'm going big . . . BIG. I have the kettle from Neils and now I'm looking for a burner to hook it up in the truck."

"Sounds like things are going great," I said.

"Some flavours are just flying off the shelf," Shard said, shaking her head like she didn't understand it. "Who is eating sage-and-onion-flavoured popcorn?"

I shrugged.

"It is a healthy, gluten-free snack alternative," Vinnie said, "for those people who are getting a muffin top from my muffin tops." He laughed at his own joke.

"What are you doing here?" Shard asked me.

"Looking for bathroom fixtures. Dad's facilities are, um, rough. He needs to fix the bathhouse up before they'll let me move in with him."

"So, you need a new throne? I think the porcelain pile is over there." Shard led the way to a spot behind some old water heaters where both sides of the path were lined by toilets of every colour. "If you squint, it almost looks like the Avenue of Sphinxes in Egypt," she said.

Shard wanted me to take the mint-green one, saying pastels were coming back in fashion, but there was no way I was sitting on something that was the colour of baby food. I opted for a plain white toilet instead.

"What about a sink?" Shard asked. We looked all around, since sinks proved hard to find, and the only one I could see was an old-fashioned square one that looked like it belonged in a museum. Didn't really matter, as long as it held water.

"And the pièce de résistance is over here," Shard called, from behind some old fencing and sheet metal.

I walked over. "I've seen one of those before," I said. "It's a water trough for cows."

"Use your imagination for once," she said, making a face and then stepping inside the trough. "This, is your new . . . bathtub."

I shook my head. "Cows had their dirty tongues in there. *No way* am I taking a bath in that."

"So, you scrub it and maybe paint it. No biggie. Let me tell you, it will totally impress Mrs. CPS. For sure she'll let you stay if you can take a *bath*."

Shard had this uncanny way of making total sense.

"Okay, but I don't even have cash to buy the toilet or sink, let alone this . . ." I waved toward the big trough.

"Bathtub," Shard finished for me.

"And I'm not sure my dad does either," I added. I knew Shard wouldn't judge statements like that. We came from the same neighbourhood.

"So, you barter."

"With what? We don't have anything to trade."

"Gold's not the only valuable thing on your grandfather's claim," she said. "You've got trees."

I scanned the junkyard, which was surrounded by a forest. "So has Flash Gordon. There are trees everywhere. Why would he want ours?"

"Because you have special ones. One's with . . ." she screwed up her face as if trying to remember something, ". . . burls."

"Burls?"

"That weird growth we saw on the tree trunk the day we planted the garden. I Googled it when we got back to Vinnie's, just to make sure it wasn't something nasty or infectious. Turns out they're just some trunk cells that forgot to stop growing, and more importantly . . ." She paused for effect. ". . . they're really valuable. Some people carve them into bowls and stuff. They can go for, like, $150 a kilogram!"

Could a massive tree wart really be worth so much? I guess in the Yukon anything is possible. At any rate, when Shard and I found Flash Gordon poking at a pile of pipes with a wooden stick, he thought the burl we described would be enough to pay for the bathroom fixtures. He wanted to be sure we didn't cut down a living tree though, because he said he was a "steward of the northern forests," whatever that means, and told us that burls didn't hurt the trees at all. I assured him the tree was already down. I was excited to hunt for more of them on the claim to give us a bit of cash, now that I knew they were valuable.

"So, you found some things, did you?" Neils said, coming over to where Flash Gordon and I were standing.

"Yup, he did. And I'm getting a burl from his father out of the deal," Gord said, rubbing his hands together. "I'll go make up the invoice."

Neils and I loaded the toilet, sink and cattle trough — I mean bathtub — into the back of his pickup. I waved goodbye to Shard, who was heading back to find Vinnie.

"Okay, in you go. Hurry up," Neils said, looking around nervously. As I walked around to the other side of the truck, I saw him pale almost to the colour of his Viking-blond hair at the sound of a *gleep*. Lucy burst out of the tall weeds at the edge of the yard, eyes locked on Neils. I've never seen anyone move so fast as Neils did in that moment. He flung open the door and dove headfirst into the truck. Unfortunately his jeans caught on the seat-belt buckle, leaving him half in and half out of the truck. He was kicking his feet to squirm into the truck while Lucy pecked at his boots. Neils was also making little yelps as he tried to free himself. I swear Lucy was looking at me and laughing in between *gleeps*. At last Gordon came out from behind a tower of car bumpers.

"Away with ya, ya daft goose," he said, and with a final *gleep* and a satisfied look on her face, Lucy waddled away. Gordon pulled Neils back out of the truck so he unhooked from the seat belt holding him hostage.

"Thanks," Neils muttered.

"You know, a few kernels and she'd be your friend for life."

"I'm not bribing vindictive poultry," Neils said, sitting with a *hrumpf* and starting the truck.

Gordon laughed, passing me the invoice while

keeping back and not touching the truck. "Suit yourself."

We drove back to Cottonwood Creek, the slick mud spraying onto the windshield up front, and my new toilet at the back. We turned down the lane to drop off the fixtures for my dad. As we got close to the cabin, I craned my neck to see if he was there, but the claim was quiet and empty. We unloaded the fixtures beside the bathhouse. I could see that the frame had been straightened with a log wedged under one corner and that some of the holes in the roof had been patched. I wished I could be here when my dad saw the new fixtures. I remembered I also had to get the burl back to Gord for payment.

"Do you have your chainsaw with you?" I asked Neils.

"Not today. Why?"

"I thought we could cut the burl out and then I'll take it to Gordon the next time we head that way."

Neils gave me a quizzical look. "Shouldn't your dad be doing that?" he asked. "After all, it's for his bathhouse and the burl is on his claim."

"Yeah, I guess. Only he doesn't know I made the deal. I don't even think he knows what a burl is. And I doubt he has a chainsaw yet." I felt my cheeks flush. I could see Neils didn't understand

I was used to doing everything for myself — and for my dad, most of the time.

"I'll give your dad the message and lend him my chainsaw, if he needs it. Come on, the dogs need some exercise."

I left reluctantly, wishing we would pass my dad coming down the lane as we left so I could tell him what I had arranged. But the only sounds I could hear out the open truck window were the creek gurgling and the wind rustling the leaves.

What I didn't hear were the words going in my dad's ears at that very moment — the ones dragging him back down.

CHAPTER 11
SHADY CHARACTERS

In the end, Neils did get permission to supervise my visits with my dad, but I didn't have a chance to see him again for several days. When Neils finally got a moment to take me over, he agreed to bring his chainsaw in case my dad wanted to borrow it to cut out the burl. But when we got there, the claim was empty. I checked the cabin. It was a bit of a mess with dirty dishes in a basin, and sheets and clothes on the floor. Maybe Dad was in a hurry to get his mining equipment? I checked the bathhouse. The fixtures were still sitting outside the door, but there was new stuff piled up beside them — some copper pipes, a box of metal clips or something and a wrench. That was encouraging. But a quick look inside showed no more work had been done on the walls or roof.

"How's the bathhouse coming?" Neils asked,

when I came back down the path. I didn't want to tell him the work had stalled. I couldn't even face that possibility. I was pinning all my hopes on the fact that Dad had turned his life around. So I lied.

"Looking okay," I said.

"Well, if he isn't here, I suggest we come back in a day or so."

I nodded. For the first time I didn't want to come back right away — I wanted to give Dad time to finish a few projects so Mrs. Olsen would be impressed the next time she drove up from Whitehorse. And so I wouldn't have to lie to Neils again.

Seeing as my visit wasn't going to happen, Neils drove us into Dawson to pick up some dog food. He bumped into Mr. Barlow, and they started chatting about the Yukon Quest sled dog race and how their training was going. There was no doubt it was going to be a long conversation, so I gestured silently to him that I was going for a walk down Second Avenue toward the ferry. Just off Second Avenue, on Deadman's Lane, I saw a familiar white truck — the Muffin Man was open for business and there was a long line out front. As I got closer, I could smell popcorn and . . . garlic? I hoped I was wrong. The sandwich board out front advertised two flavours of muffin: Moose Rack and Caribou-berry; and two flavours of gourmet popcorn: sage-onion, which Vinnie called Not Your Grandma's Stuffing, and honey-garlic, called The Bee's Knees.

"Two more Not Stuffings!" I heard Shard call from the window.

"Coming right up!" Vinnie called back.

It was amazing to see the lineup for the stinkiest popcorn I could imagine. What ever happened to good old cheese popcorn? I walked around the side of the truck and poked my head in the open kitchen door.

"I'm going to take a break, okay, Uncle Vinnie?" Shard said, seeing me.

Vinnie nodded and waved.

"Took you long enough," she said when she was outside, folding her arms.

"What do you mean?"

"My email. The one I sent two days ago telling you Fiona wanted to talk to you."

I wrinkled my nose, trying to remember the last time I opened my email. I had meant to, but with all the drama over my visits to my dad, I'd forgotten. Again.

"Seriously, Chris. READ YOUR EMAIL."

"All right, all right. I'll try to check it more often."

"If you didn't get my message, why are you here?" she asked.

"Dad wasn't on the claim for my visit, so we drove into town for dog food. What did Fiona want to talk to me about?"

Shard looked uncomfortable. "You should just go see Fiona. She dropped by earlier and said she had to pick up some more cheese for her mom at the Bonanza Market. If you hurry, you can probably still catch her.

I jogged down Second Avenue to the market. As I ran up the ramp to the doors, I saw Fiona.

"Hey, Fiona. Shard said you wanted to speak to me?" I huffed.

Fiona and I walked down to the street.

"How's your dad doing?" she asked.

I got that sinking feeling. No one asks how someone is doing unless they think there is something wrong.

"Okay, I guess. Why?"

Fiona didn't answer right away, then she said, "You know I've always been straight with you, right, kid?"

I nodded. This was not going to be good.

"Well, I was in the Dawson Hotel the other night. Your dad was there."

My shoulders dropped. This was not what I wanted to hear.

"And he was sitting with two shady characters. I didn't like the looks of them."

We fell silent. It was the worst news I could imagine. If my dad started back down the path to nightly drinking, there's no way I could go and live with him. Mrs. Olsen had made it perfectly clear that was one of the rules for my dad to get me back.

"I think he's trying to find some mining equipment," I said, straightening my shoulders. "It was probably a business meeting."

Fiona stopped right in the middle of the road. "Who do you think you're talking to here? You think I don't know sketchy people when I see them?"

I hung my head. Fiona owned a dive bar called the Bull and Brambles back in the city. My dad and his "friends" were regulars, and I had had to pull him out of there more times than I can count. If she calls someone a "shady character," you better believe she knows what she's talking about.

"Thanks for the heads-up," I said, and walked back to the muffin truck. When Shard took a break, I told her what Fiona had said.

"Oooh. That's bad."

"I know. It's bad. Real bad. But what can I do about it?"

"Nothing," Shard said.

"I can't do *nothing*."

"You can't babysit him, either."

"No," I said, sticking my chin out. "But I'll just have to make sure he has the equipment he needs to mine. If he's busy with mining, he'll be too busy to catch a ride into town to go to the bars. And once he starts to make some money, I'll be able to live with him again and keep a close eye on him."

"Mining equipment? How are you going to get that? There aren't that many burls in all of Dawson."

I didn't know what to say. It was the only thing I could think of to keep my dad on track. "Neils said he had some connections and knew people with spare sluices and stuff."

Shard shrugged. "If you think your dad will take help from Neils . . ."

I sighed. There was no guarantee of that.

"Those men better stay away from him," I said angrily. "He doesn't need new drinking buddies. If Mrs. Olsen finds out . . ."

I didn't need to finish the sentence. We both knew what was at stake.

CHAPTER 12
BREAK A LEG!

Is it wrong to be happy someone has a broken leg? I mean, I didn't want anything really bad to happen to Mrs. Olsen, but I have to admit I did a fist pump when I heard she couldn't come to Dawson for a while and that Neils would have to keep supervising my visits for now. Something was going on with my dad, and I needed time to get him back on track before she came up again.

Neils had promised to take me over again that afternoon. We had gone twice the weekend before. The first time my dad said he was sick with the flu and we couldn't visit in case he got me sick, and the other time he wasn't there. Even Neils was starting to look skeptical. I hoped I could finally tell my dad about the burl he owed Flash Gordon, but after lunch Neils got a call from his crew. They had to move their sluice plant to a new site closer to the gold, and those things weighed several tonnes. It would take their biggest dozer to drag it.

"We'll go over to see your dad tomorrow, okay?" he said, putting on his coat by the door. I nodded.

"Aren't you taking Chris with you to the claim?" Anna asked, coming into the hallway.

"No way. If that sluice tips over, or one of the cables snaps, he could be seriously hurt. Or worse."

Anna paled. "Then you be careful too," she said, as Neils waved goodbye from halfway out the door.

Anna said she was going to mend some of Neils's shirts, so I went on the computer to prove to Shard that I did check my email. But of course, the one time I remembered to look, there was nothing new. So, I opened the Wizarding World game Neils had on his computer. Sometimes I just needed to tune out real life for a while. I had just managed to breach the Cavern of Secrets when Anna popped her head in.

"Catastrophe," she said, a bit breathlessly. "Abigail Lockhart emergency texted me to say her big tabby, Percy, just ate about nine of the chicken à la king pastries she had ready for her booth at the Dawson City Music Festival. And evidence suggests he licked several others and walked on the rest. Abigail said Percy has been on the warpath since the vet made her switch him to low-fat kibble. Anyway, I promised to come and staff her booth with apple strudels until she can get another batch of chicken pastries baked. Will you be okay alone for a while?"

I nodded. "The goblins are mounting an army, and I have to plan a counterattack," I said, pointing at the screen.

"Good, good. I shouldn't be too long, unless Percy is still holding a grudge and manages to sabotage the next batch. You can call Neils down at the claim if you need something."

"I'll be fine. I'm used to being alone a lot," I said.

Anna didn't answer, but she did make a face.

"What's that on your jeans?" I asked, seeing something black crawling up her leg.

"Ah!" she screamed, brushing it off and stepping on it. "An ant. I hate ants."

She went to set out an ant trap in the back hallway. A few minutes later I heard her call goodbye as she flew out the door.

I hated to deceive Anna — she was so nice — but this was important. I had an opportunity to find out what was going on with my dad without anyone hovering over us. I knew that if I could get a few minutes alone with him, I could help him — or at least get to the bottom of whatever it was.

I closed the computer and got ready. My plan was to get to our claim the back way Neils and I had taken with the sled dogs, across the creek and then down the old path. I didn't want to take a chance on going out to the main road and being seen. It was just the Dearing luck that someone would come driving by and start asking questions.

My breath was ragged as I sprinted down the track, away from the house. The shallow creek crossing had seemed closer when we were out with the dogs. I was panting so hard by the time I reached the spot that I had to stop and catch my breath. But the idea that Neils or Anna might come home sooner than I thought motivated me to splash across the creek and start my sprint back toward Dad's cabin. I had to stop a few times to breathe, but finally I saw the clearing where Dad was going to start mining. It was empty.

Ignoring how tired I was from my run, I hurried to the cabin. I wanted to hear all my dad's plans.

I screeched to a stop when I heard a strange voice.

"Where do ya think yer goin'?"

A man stared at me from the shadow of a large

pine. His eyes were mostly hidden by the brim of a ballcap, and his crooked teeth showed through slightly parted lips. He had "Filthy Rat" written all over him. He also was a lot bigger than me. Even though I was terrified, I had to play it cool.

"Just looking for my dad."

The man's face changed from suspicion to understanding and his lips spread into a smarmy smile that scared me more than his menacing look.

"You must be Chris."

I nodded.

"Hey, Daryl," the man called over his shoulder. "Frank's kid's here."

Another man materialized from the bush. He was shorter than the first guy and his gaze shifted around as if he was on constant lookout for an attack.

"Whad'ya want?" he said, in my general direction. I wasn't sure he was talking to me though. His gaze never stayed on one thing for long.

Ballcap guy shot him a dirty look as if to say, *We gotta be nice to the kid.*

"Just saying hi to my dad," I said innocently. Truth was, I now knew the trouble with my dad. Fiona was right — it was these two shady characters: Ballcap and Shifty. I kept walking toward the cabin and tried to hide the shiver that was going up and down my back. I could feel their eyes following me and heard them whispering to each other. One thing I knew for sure . . . I had to get my dad away from these guys.

The door to the cabin was open just a bit, so I pushed on it, trying to see into the darkness.

"Dad?"

I could hear snoring in the back corner.

"DAD?"

"Hrmmm?" The figure rolled over and coughed. "Chris?"

I walked the rest of the way in. Dad looked even worse than the last time I saw him. He hadn't shaved in days, and he was skinnier than ever.

"I, uh, was just taking a break," he said slowly, sitting up. "Been working hard."

I could feel all the hope for us to be together again draining out of me. I had seen my dad looking like this too often not to recognize the signs of a hangover.

I sat down beside him on the bed. There in the tiny cabin we were surrounded by dirty dishes, dirty clothes and dirty cans. Another bad sign. Dad saw me looking around.

"I have'n had time to tidy up," he said softly, as if speaking made his head hurt.

"I don't think those guys should be here," I said quietly, worried they were listening at the door.

"No, they're my inves-sors," he said.

"Investors? Investors in what?"

"They're fronting the money for our equipment."

"What equipment?" I hadn't seen anything in the clearing when I came in.

"It's on the way."

We sat in silence for a minute while my dad rubbed his bloodshot eyes. I noticed that his shirt was stained and stank of body odour.

"What about the bathhouse? I can't come and live with you until the bathhouse is done," I said.

"Oh yeah. I been busy getting mining equipment, but it's next on my to-do list." He got up and put on his boots. I needed to try one more time.

"So, those two guys. Once the equipment comes, will they be going?"

Dad shook his head. "Nah. Dey're gonna help me. Won't be long before we're rolling in it!" He punched my shoulder for emphasis. I gave him a weak smile. When we walked back outside, Ballcap and Shifty were lurking nearby. I bet anything they had been listening.

"Daryl and Carl here have an excavator and a sluice lined up. We should be mining by the end of next week," Dad said.

I smiled at them as if I believed it.

"Well, I had better get going. It was nice meeting you," I said to them, not wanting to give away that I was onto them. I started jogging out the way I came, hoping to get back before Anna or Neils noticed I was missing. I would be in so much trouble if they found out I was visiting my dad unsupervised. But that didn't worry me as much as what was going on with our claim. I wasn't as quick as Shard at reading people, but I knew this right away: those two guys were bad news. Somehow I had to get rid of them before Mrs. Olsen got back on her feet and paid another visit to Dawson. One look at the state of the cabin and the bathhouse, or at my dad's bloodshot eyes, and I'd be in foster care for years. And if Neils and Anna couldn't or wouldn't keep me that long, I could be moved anywhere, including far away from him.

But I didn't know how to do it. How do you run off two huge men who look like they don't mind a fight, and especially when your dad won't back you up because he doesn't even recognize they are trouble? I had no idea, but I knew someone who would.

CHAPTER 13

GOLD FEVER

When I finally got back to Neils and Anna's, I slowed near the treeline to have a peek. It's a good thing I did — Anna's car was there. I backtracked into the bushes, hoping she wasn't looking out the window. What was I going to do? I decided to sneak over to the dog yard and pretend I was checking on Bullet. I came back to the house by that path and noisily entered through the back door. She didn't say anything when I gave her my story. I think she bought it. I went back to the computer, but instead of playing my game, I emailed Shard. She was my go-to friend when I needed a plan of action. Who was I kidding? She was my only friend.

The rest of the day I fooled around in Neils's workshop, using a hammer and nails to make a coat rack for my dad. Neils had given me permission to use the scrap wood piled in the corner, but the nails either bent over when I hit them or split the wood where they went in. I gave up after a while and went inside. Dad was going to have to use the nail on the wall for a while longer. I checked my email. No answer from Shard. Wasn't she always complaining that I was the one who didn't respond to messages?

Thwack!

"There's another one!" Anna yelled. "Where are these ants coming from?"

Thwack.

I helped her get rid of about six big black ants that were marching up the cupboards, across the counters and over the floors. We put six more ant traps in corners and by the back door.

"I don't think I can take it anymore," she said, wringing her hands. "I HATE ants."

I looked at her sideways. "Didn't Neils tell me you once scared off a black bear with a hair dryer and a cheese grater?"

Anna put her hands on her hips. "Bears get all up in your face and let you know who they are and what they want. You hear them coming; you smell them too. They don't crawl into your sugar bowl and sneak around on baseboards waiting until you fall asleep to camp out on your eyelids."

Anna started rubbing her arms as if she felt ants crawling on them. I went back to my computer game, but to be honest, I kept scratching at my arms too.

At supper, Neils asked if I wanted to come with him to his claim in the morning. I said yes right away because the truth was I didn't have the heart to go back to the Dearing claim and see those two Filthy Rats up to no good. At least not until I had a plan to do something about it.

I checked my email one last time before bed. Nothing.

I checked again before we left for Neils's claim the next morning. Still nothing. Boy was I going to have fun ripping a strip off Shard the way she did to me when I didn't answer.

Usually the mining operation on the claim was an orchestra of motors, gears and pulleys all grinding, chugging and humming. Today it was quiet.

"We found some interesting artifacts this week that I'll show you later. Leo, Dave and I have to fix the shaker deck first," Neils said, getting out of the truck.

We walked over to the sluice. I had no idea what a shaker deck was or how you fixed it, but it looked like a big job.

"Can I do some panning?" I asked Neils, who was arming himself with some oversized tools from the work shed.

"What?" he asked. He seemed a bit distracted.

"Yes. Just stay away from the sluice here. Could be dangerous."

"Can I keep what I find?"

"Sure."

"Okay," I said, grabbing a pan from the work shed and wandering away from the sluice. I looked at the mine site and wondered where I should get dirt to pan. I tried to channel my granddad and figure out where the gold might be. I got nothing. So, I headed to the edge of the pond behind the sluice. I pushed some muddy dirt into my pan and then filled it with water. I tried to remember how Leo showed me to do it, shaking the pan and then letting the water wash the rocks and soil from the top, leaving the heavy gold to sink to the bottom. It took a long time and my arms were getting sore, but I was finally down to the black magnetite grains. Leo had told me that when I got to the black, it was the final layer and the gold would be underneath.

I swirled the pan to move the magnetite to the side and looked for what Leo called "colours." I swirled and looked and swirled and looked closer and then there they were. Three tiny golden grains glowing in the sun. My heart skipped a beat. Gold. It was beautiful. I carefully carried the pan over to the work shed. I needed a jar or something to put my gold in.

"What are you rummaging around for?" Dave asked, coming in and wiping grease from his hands.

"I need a container for my gold."

"You found some gold?"

"Yes, look."

"You're right. Three colours here, and I see one more tiny one over in the crease there."

I looked where he was pointing. There it was! Dave found a little glass jar that used to have jam in it. He dipped his finger into the pan and let the gold stick to it so he could pull it out and shake it into the jar. He put the lid on when all four were in there.

"This is not bad for your first try," Dave said. "Where did you get the pay dirt?"

I pointed to the edge of the pond. "Right over there."

"Uh-oh," Dave said. I watched him go out and say something to Neils, who came striding back.

"Hey, Chris, can you show me where you were panning?" Neils said.

I walked him over to the spot. Neils's frown deepened.

"Did I do something wrong?" I asked.

Neils shook his head. "No, but you were panning from the tailings pond."

"Oh. Is that bad?"

"It's bad that there is still gold in the tailings — the leftovers from sluicing. It means the sluice isn't catching the gold properly. But, thanks to you, we know now and can make some adjustments as we fix the shaker deck. So, thanks." He gave me a thump on my back.

"Can I keep panning?" I asked, holding my jar of gold dust up to the sunlight for another look.

Neils laughed. "It was bound to happen."

"What?"

"You've got gold fever."

I flushed. Is this what gold fever felt like? The tingling to get back out there and dig through the dirt to see those shiny pieces at the bottom of the pan? If so, then I for sure had a bad case of it.

I got to keep panning until the sluice was fixed. After that the tailings pond was too dangerous because that's where the sluice deposited the soil and rocks from the pay dirt. As Leo brought the sluice mats to the shed for a cleanup, I showed him my loot.

"All you have to do is fill a jar like this," he said, pointing to a Mason jar on the shelf in the gold room, "and you'd have about $100,000."

I looked at the Mason jar and then back at my jam jar. Working all afternoon, I had found about fifteen tiny flakes of gold dust. I couldn't wait to help my dad mine our claim. I wanted to run my hands through a whole pile of gold and know it was ours.

"So, about how much would a nugget be worth?" I asked.

"Depends on how much it weighs."

I tried to picture the size of my granddad's nugget. "Let's say the size of a cough drop."

"Hmm. Sounds like it would be about an ounce. The price of gold goes up and down, but right now it's about $1,900 an ounce."

I tried not to look disappointed or Leo might ask why I wanted to know. But I was pretty sure that wouldn't be enough money for even a second-hand sluice. It could buy a stove and another bed for the cabin though. And enough frozen pizzas that we would never have to eat pickles and crackers for supper again.

"I have something else for you too," Leo said, waving at me to follow him to his car. From the back seat he pulled a plastic bag containing a file folder full of papers.

"Is that stuff about my granddad?" I asked.

Leo nodded. "Margie made copies of any reports or articles about the incident."

"Thanks, and thank Margie too," I said, remembering the manners my mom used to drill into me.

"I hope it's what you're looking for," he said.

"So do I." I trembled a little as I carried the

bag. Would it have a clue to clear my granddad's name, and maybe the Dearing name too? Or would it be just another embarrassing reason to change mine when I hit eighteen?

Back at Neils and Anna's house, I had to wait until after supper to take out the file and open it in my room.

The first page was a photocopy of the Yukon Gold Company's employee records from 1941. I ran a finger down the list of names done in fancy writing. There it was:

Wallace Dearing *Hansen Street, Dawson*
Stern d. *$80.00 the month*

An address! This must be where he lived before he got the claim. I wanted to go right now and see where it was and stand on the spot and look at what he looked at when he came out of his house each morning. Below his address it read *Stern d.* I didn't know what that was. I stuffed the envelope under my mattress and went to find Neils.

"On a dredge, stern d would stand for stern decker," Neils said, when I asked him.

"What did they do?"

"Well, stern means the back of a ship. So, the stern decker worked at the back of the dredge. Watched the stacker and the tailings pile. Why do you want to know that?"

"My granddad was a stern decker."

I saw Neils and Anna exchange looks.

"Who told you that?" he asked.

"I, uh, my dad told me once." Don't ask me why I didn't tell them about the papers Leo gave me. It's just that after living with secrets for so long, you get to know when something's not right. I figured Neils and Anna must know about my granddad and the theft and were trying to keep it from me. I would have to figure out the rest of the story by myself. I went back to my room and looked at the next page. It was a newspaper article from the *Dawson Daily News*.

Theft at Dredge No. 2

Sam Greenwald of the Yukon Gold Company reports that a quantity of gold has been stolen from the gold room aboard Dredge No. 2. Mr. Greenwald has contacted the Royal Canadian Mounted Police to begin an investigation.

The article went on to say that the suspect was an employee of the dredge who had not been seen for three days. Well, I knew who *that* was.

"Chris! Supper!"

The rest would have to wait until later. I doubted I would sleep that night. I needed to know everything the old newspapers and records could tell me.

CHAPTER 14

HIT THEM WHERE IT HURTS

"Don't just throw it, shake it on carefully," Shard said, grabbing the shaker from my hands and showing me for the third time how to put topping on a bowl of popcorn.

"Who is buying oregano-kale popcorn, anyway?" I asked, not really convinced it mattered how I coated the popcorn with the hideous green mixture.

"Put kale in anything and people think it's health food. Ladies are buying it by the bucketful. Vinnie calls it his Fountain of Youth flavour."

"I don't always understand people," I said.

I had convinced Neils to drive me into town by using the story that Vinnie had asked for my help. Really, I needed to get some time to talk to Shard. She never did answer my email. That was probably because when I checked my mail, I noticed it wasn't in my sent folder. Seems I never pressed the *send* button after I wrote it. I didn't admit that to Shard, mind you. Instead I emailed her again, and she answered right away. She told me she had to help Vinnie the next day and to meet her at the food truck. So, I arranged it because I needed the help of her quick mind in coming up with a plan to get those Filthy Rats away from my dad. But so far all I had time for was shaking green gunk on popcorn and burning my fingertips pulling hot muffin trays out of the oven.

"What *is* that disgusting smell?"

Shard and I spun around to see Fiona at the back door of the truck.

"Hi, Fi!" Vinnie called from behind us. "Come on in!"

The food truck isn't the roomiest place, so Shard and I were grateful when Vinnie told us to take a break and get some fresh air. Besides, Vinnie and Fiona seemed *very* happy to see each other, and I certainly didn't want to watch *that*.

Shard and I walked down to Front Street to get a snack at the General Store.

"I need some advice," I said finally.

"Uh-huh," Shard said, not looking surprised at all.

"Those two guys Fiona saw with my dad at the bar, I think they're the same two who were out at the claim. He's calling them his 'investors,' but I've got a bad feeling about them."

Shard stopped walking. "They're at the claim?"

I nodded.

"That's really bad. I think they were deliberately trying to get your dad drinking again."

"Why would they do that?" I asked. "What good is a drunken miner?"

Shard stopped and put her hands on her hips. "Can you think of a better way to get the location of the gold out of him and then keep him out of the way while they steal all the loot?"

My head started to hurt. Why hadn't I thought of that? They could pull thousands of dollars worth of gold out of the ground and pocket it, and Dad would never even know. The Dearing curse of being swindled was alive and well, and I was watching it in action.

I started walking again, only faster. "I need to do something!" I said, my stomach twisting into knots.

Shard put a hand on my shoulder to slow me down. "No. *We* need to do something. This is a job for more than one person."

Have I mentioned how happy I was to have my best friend here again?

"So, what can we do?"

There was a pause as we walked down the

road, kicking at loose stones.

"Let me think on it," she said finally.

We got to the store and grabbed a snack that wasn't stinky popcorn, then started back.

"I think I need to see the situation for myself," Shard said. "Every time Vinnie and I go to water the garden, we don't see anyone. Maybe because we go so stupid early in the morning. Vinnie wants to catch the breakfast-muffin crowd, small as it is. If I get a ride out to your place tomorrow afternoon, could we go over to your dad's claim?"

"Well," I said, glancing over at her, "not officially."

"Yeah, whatever. But can we get over there?"

"I'm not supposed to be there unsupervised."

"So, we'll have Vinnie come. I'll tell him it's a garden emergency. I'll say some moose are eating all his kale."

I shook my head. "Vinnie's not approved. Only Neils or Mrs. Olsen can take me."

"Pfft," Shard said. "Bureaucracy is for people with more time and money than we have. I'll just have Vinnie drop me off then."

I thought about it. Anna was going into town for a horticultural society meeting, and Neils had said he was heading to his claim tomorrow and wanted me to come along.

"I guess I could pretend to not be feeling well so they'll leave me home."

"Now you're talking like a Sunnyview Terrace tenant."

When I lived in the same crappy apartment building as Shard, we used to excuse a lot of things we did, like Dumpster diving for used furniture or scouring alleys for empty beer bottles to turn them in for the deposit, by saying it was the "Sunnyview way" of doing things. I guess lying about being sick, sneaking over to the Dearing claim, and trying to trick two swindlers was the "Sunnyview way" of surviving in the Yukon.

"Okay, but you'll have to keep out of sight somewhere until Neils and Anna leave."

"No problem. I'll just hang out with the moose in the bushes."

"Don't even joke about that," I said. "I still need to get you back for your 'onions ward off moose' disaster. You almost got me killed!"

"You're exaggerating. I'll see you tomorrow."

* * *

I am not normally known as a great actor but my performance the next morning was Oscar worthy. I decided to go with the invisible "bad headache." That way I didn't have to fake a fever or pretend I was going to throw up. Sometimes when I did the fake-gagging thing, it made me feel like I was *really* going to throw up.

I stayed in my room with the blind down until I heard Neils's truck leave. Anna came in with some water and a pill, which I told her I'd take if my headache didn't ease off soon. Then I heard her car start up and go down the driveway. I hopped out of bed, grabbed my jacket, put on my shoes, and slipped outside.

"Shard," I called. I walked down the lane a bit. "Shard!" I called again.

She emerged from some shrubs waving her arms around. "These mosquitoes are as big as bats. Do you have repellent or something?"

I went back in the house and grabbed the bottle Anna kept by the door. "I don't think this is good for you," I said, covering her in a fog of chemicals.

"Being bitten every few seconds isn't either. Who knows what they're infecting me with — malaria, Zika, dengue fever."

"Those are tropical diseases," I said. "There's none of that in the Yukon."

"You never know," she said, still swatting.

"Come on, let's go. If I'm caught doing this, I'll be in deep, deep trouble." At the very least I was sure Mrs. Olsen would reverse her decision to let Neils supervise my visits.

"Where are you going?" Shard asked, starting down the lane.

"We're going the back way. If anyone sees me on the main road, they'll tell Neils or Anna for sure, or even Mrs. Olsen, and then I can kiss being with my dad full-time goodbye."

"So, back through the bush, where there are blackflies as well as mosquitoes?"

I didn't even answer. I just took off down the path. I could hear Shard's footsteps behind me. After the long trek beside Cottonwood Creek, we splashed across the shallow part and headed back down the other side toward the cabin.

"Wait up!" Shard yelled. "I've been cooped up in a food truck for three weeks. I'm not exactly in shape for a cross-country run."

"Shhhh," I said, coming to a stop. "The clearing is just up ahead. I don't know if they're mining today or what."

I held my breath, listening. Then I heard it . . . voices.

I looked over my shoulder at Shard. She nodded and pointed off to the right. We crept forward and peered through the brush. I saw movement ahead of us — a flash of red through the branches and leaves.

I went a little closer, crouching in an uncomfortable position and communicating with Shard by using silent gestures. Red shirt turned out to be the guy I called Ballcap. He was working on some sort of rusty piece of machinery. It didn't look at all like Neils's sluice. In the middle it had a big cylinder that was full of small holes. Shifty was there too, and he seemed to be trying to turn it.

"It's completely rusted together," Shifty said to Ballcap. "I can't get it to budge."

"Hit it with a hammer," Ballcap said. "We have to get this working before Frank comes by."

"Don't worry. He's snoring in his bunk. Probably won't wake up for hours yet."

"I'm going to get some oil to loosen up these gears. Wish we'd been able to buy something that hadn't been sitting in a field for fifty years. This is a piece of junk."

"Junk or not, it's all we have," Shifty said. "We'll be able to buy whatever we want once we get this plan in motion."

Ballcap grunted and then turned to go. Just then, my knee gave out and I fell forward with a grunt. I had to grab the bush in front of me to not go face first into the dirt.

"What was that?" Shifty called to Ballcap. "Do you think it's a bear?"

We froze as Ballcap scanned the area. "I don't know. Want me to check?"

In a panic, I looked at Shard. She rolled her eyes and picked up a rock, and when Ballcap and Shifty were looking the other way, she threw it into the bushes away from us. The Filthy Rats spun around at the noise. Shifty went to the bushes and moved them aside a little.

"Probably just a squirrel or something."

Ballcap shrugged and walked toward the cabin. Shifty went back to the machine and started smacking the wheels under the cylinder.

I signalled to Shard for us to go back, and we quietly timed our steps to the clanging of Shifty's swings.

We moved faster as we got farther away from the clearing. We didn't speak until we had splashed across the creek and were headed back to Neils and Anna's house.

"Well?" I asked.

Shard sighed. "Just scaring them off isn't good enough. They'll either come back or some other guys will think your dad's an easy mark and take their place. So, no use pretending the place is haunted, or under a curse, or stalked by a giant grizzly."

"How about sabotage? They can't mine if they can't get that rust bucket of a machine to work."

Shard squinted up at the sky. "Could be fun, but if we get caught . . ."

Right. I would no longer be a foster child; I'd be a juvenile delinquent.

"How about replacing all the booze with water. That way they couldn't get my dad drunk."

Shard shook her head. "They'd catch on pretty fast and just go out and buy more."

"Food poisoning?"

"I like your style, but no. We have to hit them where it hurts."

"Which is where?"

"Money. Gold. We have to snarl them in paperwork. If the government suspects they are doing something illegal, they'd be *happy* to put a stop-work order on the place."

"But wouldn't that mean my dad can't mine either, once we get rid of them?"

"Hmmm. Good point."

"But I like the part about stopping them from mining my dad's gold. I've learned a lot from going to Neils's claim and watching his system. You know what is critical to gold mining?"

"Shovels? Pans? Overalls? Plaid shirts?"

I shot her a dirty look. "Water. You need water to mine." Neils had explained how important water was when he showed me how the sluice ran.

Shard looked confused. "For what? Rinsing your dirty hands? Washing muddy boots?"

Now I got a turn to roll my eyes. "No, to wash the gold out of the pay dirt and off the gravel. Sluices need water. A lot of it."

"All we have to do is stop them getting water? So, like, build a dam in the creek? *That* should be easy."

If it took building a dam to get those guys away from my dad, I would do it. But I remembered something else. "Right after the Dearing claim was back in our hands, thanks to Fiona registering it for me, Neils picked up some paperwork that I needed. In it was an application for a water licence."

"What do you need that for?"

"Neils said if you use over a certain amount of water for sluicing, you have to have a licence. For sure that size of sluice will need more than the limit."

"So, did you get a licence for the claim?"

I made a face. "I'm too young and my forging skills are only so-so."

"Didn't the swindlers who owned the claim before you already have a water licence on the place?"

"Probably, but when the claim lapsed, so did the licence. Those Filthy Rats need to get a water licence from the Water Board or they can't sluice. And the whole process takes time. They're slimy enough that they would probably try to go ahead and sluice without one but not if they know their neighbour might report them. We need to make things difficult for them and delay them. Maybe long enough for them to give up and go somewhere else."

We could see Neils's house through the trees. "It could work," Shard said. "But it's not a slam dunk."

"I think it's as close as we're going to get," I said.

"So, food poisoning as a backup?"

We fist bumped. Shard texted Vinnie to pick her up and started down the lane to the main road.

"Hey, wait," she said. "Do you think Neils will agree to back you up on this? What if he just wants to mind his own business and look the other way?"

I hadn't thought of that. I didn't know how much I could trust Neils where my dad was concerned.

"I'm going to have to make sure he doesn't."

CHAPTER 15

PLAYING BY THE RULES

"What do you mean, you want me to threaten your dad with going to the Water Board on him for not having a licence?" Neils asked, when I finally got up the nerve to talk to him about my plan.

"Not threaten, just make it clear you expect everyone to play by the rules. And it's not my dad; it's those two other guys. I think they're bad news," I said.

"What two guys?"

"They call themselves his investors. But I think they're just trying to rob him of the gold. Fiona saw them with my dad in town. Even she called them shady characters."

Neils rubbed his bushy blond beard. "Having investors is pretty common, you know. Mining's expensive."

"Yeah, but I don't think they really are. They

bought some rusty fifty-year-old machine with a cylinder full of holes."

"How do you know that?"

"Uh, Shard told me she saw it when they went to water the garden the other day." I was lying again, but I really felt I had to.

"That's a trommel. It's used to separate the gold from larger stones."

"Whatever it is, it's in such bad shape they can't get it to move. I just know they're trying to swindle my dad." I was so upset I was almost shaking.

"Your dad's a grown man, Chris. I'm sure he can take care of himself . . ."

"No. He can't. That's why they took me away from him. He couldn't take care of himself, let alone me. And now our one chance is slipping away. If they can't mine, they'll leave. I just know it." My voice cracked as I got the words out.

Neils looked at me for a moment.

"Okay. Okay. I'll make sure they're aware they need a water licence. But I'm not sure it will make a difference."

I started to breathe again. "Thanks, Neils."

"I know how much you want this to work out with your dad. And so do I." He put a hand on my shoulder. I turned my head so he wouldn't see me fighting back tears. I was so relieved. I would just have to make sure Dad started the application process right away so that he could be mining as soon as the Filthy Rats were gone.

Neils took me over for a visit that afternoon. I was nervous. I worried that my dad might get so discouraged from this setback that he spiralled down even more. But I had to believe that once Ballcap and Shifty were gone, Dad would bounce back.

I had to.

When we got there, I checked the cabin, wondering if Dad would be sleeping. But it was empty. I walked to the bathhouse. The fixtures weren't outside anymore. I was excited. But when I took another look, they had just been moved inside — nothing else had been done. My stomach dropped again.

Neils and I walked toward the clearing, where we could hear some activity. It seemed like Ballcap and Shifty had got the machine working because it was squeaking and squealing as it slowly rotated. My dad stood up as we approached.

"Hey, Chris," he said, when he saw me. He was wearing a wide-brimmed hat and sunglasses, so I couldn't see his eyes, but he gave me a wide smile.

I ran over. "How's it going?" I asked.

"Just about ready to go," he said. "We're testing the trommel and just about to hook up the pump."

I looked over at Neils, who raised an eyebrow.

I smiled at my dad. "Great. Glad things are getting going. I'm surprised you got your water licence so quickly."

Out of the corner of my eye, I could see Ballcap and Shifty spin around and stare at us.

"I don't need a licence," Dad said. "I have a creek."

"Uh, yeah, I guess you didn't know that even having a creek still means you need a licence."

There was silence. Dad looked over to where Neils had plopped himself down on a log.

"Granddad never had a licence," he said.

I felt a wave of panic wash over me. "I guess things weren't as official back then."

I followed Dad's gaze to Ballcap and Shifty, who were walking over to Neils. Uh-oh.

"So, what's this about a water licence?" Ballcap asked Neils. Neils stood up and his Viking height made him tower over Ballcap, who had to tilt his head back to see Neils's face.

"Standard practice," Neils said. "Government mandate."

I think Ballcap was struggling to understand Neils's big words.

"Never heard of it before," Ballcap snarled.

Neils shrugged. "I don't make the rules."

Shifty went over to Neils and pasted a fake smile on his face. "I'm sure we can find a way around this. We're all gentlemen here."

Neils tilted his head as if he wanted to say, "Are we?" But he didn't. Instead he said, "I don't make the rules, but I've been a miner here long enough to know that you don't mess with government officials. If you get on their bad side, they will hound you for every tiny thing until your operation is paralyzed. And I'm not interested in finding ways around regulations."

He folded his arms. Conversation over.

Ballcap and Shifty looked furious. They came over to where my dad and I were standing.

"Can we talk to you for a minute?" they asked my dad.

Dad gave a nod and motioned for me to move away. I walked around the back of the sluice where I was out of sight but could still hear them.

"You gotta talk to him," Shifty said to my dad. "Without water we're not sluicing and we're gonna walk away from all this. I know lots of people up here are sluicing without a licence. If this guy keeps his mouth shut, we could be mining tomorrow."

"Without our equipment," Ballcap added, "your

mining season is over. How do you plan on repaying the money you owe us if you don't get any gold?"

I imagined my dad wringing his hands. "I'll work this out. I promise. You guys let me handle it and you just start stripping the overburden."

"You better," Shifty said.

I heard them walk away. I came out from behind the sluice to see Dad wiping sweat from his forehead.

"Dad?"

"Not now, Chris. I've got a crisis here." Dad marched over to Neils, who had gone back to lounging on the log. "So, is this how you want to play this?"

"Play?" Neils said, red creeping up his neck. "You think this is a game?"

Dad looked around to see if Shifty and Ballcap were nearby. "You are putting me in a dangerous position."

Neils folded his arms. "I think you put yourself there. I'm not concerned with your, um, partners. I'm concerned with you getting in trouble with the Yukon Water Board. You think those two hoodlums are scary? Try having your operation shut down for months, tangled up in red tape while you try to prove to the government you followed the rules." Neils got up. "You better think long and hard about how you're going to proceed. Think how it will affect you, your mine and . . ." Neils looked over at me, ". . . your family."

Dad's shoulders drooped. Neils walked back to his truck. I went over to my dad, who was looking off into the distance.

"I guess I'll see you in a few days?" I said.

My dad nodded absently.

"You'll be here, right?" I asked.

Dad looked up, a flicker of pain across his eyes. "I'm sorry I've missed your last few visits," he said, almost in a whisper. "I've been so busy trying to get parts and get this mine running and . . . and other stuff."

"I know. It's just, I miss seeing you. I thought once you got up here it'd be like it was before."

Dad pulled me into his shoulder. "Me too." Then he lifted my chin so he could look into my eyes. "And it will. I promise."

I gave him a smile, but it was a struggle. I wanted so desperately to believe him, but I didn't want to get my hopes up.

Neils and I drove back to the house in silence. I felt horribly guilty and sure hoped this was going to work.

"Can you give me a hand with the dogs today?" Neils asked.

"Sure," I said. Bullet was the best distraction. I spent the afternoon running the dogs on the wagon with Neils. We practiced going up and down hills, making sure I braked lightly going downhill so the sled didn't hit the dogs. It was exhilarating to feel their strength and power as we flew along. I let out a laugh as we went over a bump and my feet came off the wagon floor for just a second. It struck me then that I hadn't had this much fun in a long time.

* * *

After supper I went to my room and pulled out the file on my granddad. As I reread the final report by an Inspector Starnes of the RCMP, I wondered if there was a tiny detail I might have missed.

In the matter of the investigation of the theft from the gold room aboard Dredge No. 2, a quantity of gold dust and nuggets was reported missing on August 9. The suspect, stern decker Wallace Dearing, was seen entering the room just before the weekly cleanup. When the Yukon Consolidated Gold Company representative arrived to collect the gold, he noticed a quantity of gold missing from the normal weekly total, and a search was made for said suspect. It later came to my attention that on the evening of August 12, Mr. Dearing attempted to sell gold to gold buyer Mr. James Stanfield. Although a full search of the area was made, Mr. Dearing had disappeared before we arrived and a warrant is issued for his arrest.

I closed the file again. I imagined what Granddad was thinking right then. Was his breath coming in gasps as he ran through the wilderness, dodging moose and bears? Did he have to hide out? Was he scared? I would have been.

I lay back on my bed and listened to the rain pelt the roof. The creek would be high and fast tomorrow. Something else was pulling at the corners of my mind but I just couldn't pin it down, some detail that was bothering me. What was it? I tried to go over everything that had happened in the day, but it was no use.

If only I had known that detail was the key to everything, maybe I would have tried to stay awake to figure it out.

CHAPTER 16

HEARTBREAK HILL

It seemed like everyone in Dawson was out to watch the Midnight Dome Run. The yearly foot race to the top of Dome Hill, which rose up behind Dawson, had been postponed twice because of all the rain that had rolled in across the Ogilvie Mountains in July. It had been pretty wet so far this summer. Dawsonites are tough, but the road was too slick for runners, race officials and spectators to get up to the top safely, especially with no guardrails on the sharp turns. So, today was the re-race. Luckily even though it was August, it was still light out at midnight. We all gathered downtown by the Palace Grand Theatre to see the runners off. Then we were going to drive to the top of Dome Hill to wait at the finish line. Anna had baked some scones for post-race refreshments and we had to deliver them.

"Did Anna say what kind of scones she baked?" Neils asked me quietly, when Anna was busy talking to Mrs. Simms, the volunteer co-ordinator.

"Cranberry something or other," I said.

"Ooooh, cranberry-lemon, I bet." He looked over at the truck, where Anna's scones were in a box on the seat. "I wonder if she'd notice . . ."

As if she sensed what Neils was thinking, Anna turned around and stared at him. She strode over, a steely look in her eye. "If you try to scoff one of those scones, Neils Amundson," she said, "I'll cut your hands off."

"Would they really miss just one scone?" he wheedled.

"Okay, you can have one . . ."

Neils's eyes lit up.

". . . if you run the race. They'll be on the 'Runner Recovery' table at the finish line."

Neils's face fell. "Are there any left at home?"

"Nope."

"I'll see if I can borrow some running shoes," he muttered, walking away.

Anna leaned over to me. "I kept a few back for his lunch," she said, in a low voice. "But don't tell him that. I would give anything to see those pale white legs of his in a pair of shorts."

We both laughed at the thought of it. Neils

had a huge stride with his long legs, but I had never once seen him break into so much as a jog, except when trying to get away from Lucy Goosey, of course. And I'd also never seen him in anything but jeans and workboots.

Then I saw Shard in the crowd. "Where's Vinnie?" I asked, catching up to her.

"He's back at his house looking for running shoes for Neils. Any idea why Neils needs Vinnie's shoes?"

"Cranberry-lemon scones," I said, and told her what Anna had done.

"I would pay to see that," Shard said, giggling.

A few minutes later, we were standing with Neils and Anna when Vinnie trotted over. In his hands were a pair of brown suede running shoes that had seen better days.

"Look what I found!" he said, holding them up. "You're in luck, Neils! I found my runners, and look what else . . ." He held up a pair of bright red short-shorts with white piping on the seams. They were straight out of those hilarious old workout videos you can watch online.

Neils froze, all the colour draining from his face. Anna turned away, her shoulders shaking with silent laughter.

Neils looked from the shoes to Anna and back to the shorts. He made one last attempt to prevent utter humiliation. "Are you sure not even a small one fell off the tray onto the counter?" he asked, in a voice of desperation.

We couldn't hold it in any longer. Anna and I laughed so hard there were tears running down our faces. Neils, realizing he was being had, started laughing too, then gave Anna a kiss on the cheek and me a slap on the shoulder.

At that moment I happened to look up the street. There, standing on the boardwalk and looking our way, was my dad. I saw his gaunt shoulders drooping and the sadness in his eyes, and all the laughter drained out of me. Just then Ballcap and Shifty came up to him, and Shifty put his arm around my dad and pulled him into the Dawson Hotel. My dad turned his head for one more look my way. I lifted my hand in a little wave as he went inside.

"Who's manning the food truck, Uncle Vinnie?" Shard asked, bringing my attention back to the race. "I thought you said this was prime time for business with everyone down here for the start of the run."

Vinnie blushed a little. Uh-oh. I knew what that meant.

"Fiona's giving me a hand," he said. "I had better get back and, uh, help." The blush deepened and even his ears were pink. "I promised some free samples for the finish-line table."

Anna told him we would take Shard up with us. Shard looked relieved, and I didn't blame her. Vinnie and Fiona together in a small space was a recipe for lovey-dovey behaviour.

Once the runners started off, we all piled into the truck.

"Don't sit on the scones!" Anna said.

"If we squish one, can we eat it?" Shard asked, winking at me.

"No!"

I held on as Neils careened around the twists and turns up Dome Hill.

"It might have been safer to join the runners," Shard whispered, being flung almost in my lap as Neils yanked the steering wheel left.

"There's Heartbreak Hill," Neils said, pointing out the window at a particularly steep section.

"Why's it called that?"

"Lots of runners give up there," Neils said. "And let's hope a lot do today."

"That's a terrible thing to say." Anna admonished him. "Why would you want that to happen?"

Neils looked over at her and grinned. "Might be some scones leftover, then."

Anna swatted his arm.

When we got to the top, Neils parked a little

too close to the edge, if you ask me. I got out carefully, peeking at how steep the slope back down to Dawson was. I backed away, hoping Neils remembered to put the parking brake on.

After a while Vinnie and Fiona roared up on the Ducati. Roped to Vinnie's back was a garbage bag filled to the brim with popcorn samples. Shard and I walked over to help untie Vinnie's bundle.

"Where's your bike?" Shard asked her uncle.

"Needs a tune-up," he said. Fiona snorted.

"Hey, kid," Fiona said, turning to me. "You keeping out of trouble?"

I thought about how I had lied about being sick and snuck over to my dad's claim for an unsupervised visit, and about how I was trying to sabotage the Filthy Rats' operation.

"Not really," I said.

"Glad to hear it," she said, smiling. Then the look on her face changed like shutters had been closed over a window. I spun around. Anna had walked toward us, carrying the box of scones.

"Well, see you around, Chris," Fiona said, walking away as Anna took the scones to the table with the *Runner Recovery* sign on it.

"What was *that* all about?" Shard asked me.

"I dunno."

"Hmm," Shard said. I knew that look on her

face. She wouldn't rest until she got all the details on the deal with Anna and Fiona.

"So, what's going on with your dad?" she asked, changing the subject.

I didn't tell her I had seen him going into the hotel before the race started. "Neils told him and the Filthy Rats that they needed a water licence."

"How did that go over?"

"Shifty and Ballcap were really mad. Dad was suspicious. He said Granddad never needed one. I told him things had changed."

Shard nodded. "Good work. Still, I'm keeping some out-of-date yogourt in Vinnie's fridge, just in case."

We hung around to see the first of the runners arrive and then I said goodbye to Shard and headed back home with Neils and Anna. I hadn't told Shard how guilty I felt about sabotaging my dad's mining season and possibly my chances of living with him anytime soon. I knew she'd just say it was better than letting him be swindled, so I didn't bother. I felt a little smug too, that my plan had worked so well.

I forgot that I was a Dearing and nothing was ever that easy.

CHAPTER 17

LIARS, CHEATS AND FOOLS

Mrs. Olsen told Anna on the phone that she had a walking cast on now, so she was hiring a driver and coming to Dawson. My stomach clenched just thinking about it. I guess it was because I knew she held all the power over my future with my dad. It didn't help that I hadn't been over to see him for about a week because Neils had some emergencies at his claim and couldn't take me.

A few days ago I went with Neils to help out, and other than me just getting in the way, it was sort of awkward. Leo kept looking at me with such pity. He must have read the documents on my granddad's theft. I didn't know what to say to Leo, so I just smiled like being part of a loser family was fine with me. I hoped things would get back to normal soon because I liked panning for gold, even if I had still only found a few flakes.

But today they were moving the sluice plant again, and Neils said it was too dangerous for me to go to his claim. I tried to focus on feeding the dogs and not the gnawing worry that when we went over to my dad's later, those two thugs would have messed him up so bad that Mrs. Olsen would tell me I could never go back to live with him.

Bullet jumped up at me as I came over with his breakfast, and when I bent down to put his bowl in its holder, he licked my ear. I wondered when Neils would trust me enough to take them out by myself.

When I went back to the house, Anna was sprinkling powder just outside the back door.

"Is that salt? Is this place haunted?" I asked. I knew from the ghost-hunting shows I used to watch that if you sprinkle salt around the perimeter of your house, spirits wouldn't cross it.

"I wish it were ghosts. They'd be less trouble than those horrible ants that just won't leave me alone!"

"So, what is that stuff?" Looking closer, I could see it wasn't exactly white like salt but had a slightly green tint and a familiar smell.

"Um, well actually Abigail Lockhart recommended this oregano-kale mixture."

Oregano-kale? Where had I heard of that before?

"You mean, like Vinnie's Fountain of Youth

gourmet popcorn?" I asked.

Anna flushed a little and nodded. "Abigail says she just pulverizes it in her blender and sprinkles it all around her garden. The ants have disappeared. I figured it was worth a try. Everyone around town is using it."

I wondered if Vinnie knew his gourmet popcorn wasn't flying out the window because it was a delicious, nutritious snack but because it was helping with Dawson City's ant problem. I tried to imagine what the honey-garlic popcorn was being used for.

Maybe to scare away vampire bees?

By lunch I was so worried about what I would find at the claim that I almost couldn't choke down my grilled cheese sandwich. And I tensed when I heard a car come up the lane. She was here.

Mrs. Olsen had a hundred questions for me as we made the short drive over. I tried to answer, but all I could think about was what we might find when we got there.

"Something wrong, Chris?" Mrs. Olsen asked, as we pulled up near the cabin.

"N . . . no. Why?"

"Because I asked you if you'd made friends with any local children you might go to school with in the fall and you mumbled something about popcorn?"

"Oh, sorry. It's, uh, been a busy week." I craned my neck to try to get an idea of what we were facing. The claim looked empty. I just knew we would find my dad inside the cabin, snoring on the bed. I hoped Mrs. Olsen didn't see my hand shake as I opened the car door. I sprinted to the cabin, figuring maybe I could get my dad upright before Mrs. O hobbled over.

I flung the cabin door open without knocking.

My dad wasn't there but Shifty and Ballcap were. When I came inside, they spun around. They had the same look on their faces as I had when I got caught trying to forge my dad's signature on a test.

"Where's my dad?"

"Oh, he, uh, took my truck and nipped into town," Shifty said.

"But he knew I was coming," I said, hearing the shuffling of Mrs. Olsen coming up behind me.

"Your father isn't here?" she asked me, looking around.

"I'm sure he'll be back in a minute," Ballcap said.

"And who are you?" Mrs. O asked, pulling out her clipboard.

"We're his business partners," Shifty said.

Mrs. O made a note on the form.

"Where did Frank say he was going?" Mrs. O asked Shifty and Ballcap.

"Uh, he didn't say," Ballcap said. "Maybe he scarpered off. We're having trouble getting started mining. I doubt we'll see much result this season."

It didn't sound right that my dad would take off and not say anything . . . He knew we were coming today. I didn't believe he would just throw away his chance to have me back. That wasn't my dad at all. I squinted at Ballcap. He gave me a steely look back. I suddenly knew what was going on. He and Shifty didn't want me to come and live here because then I would be able to keep an eye on things and keep my dad on the straight and narrow. It would be hard to swindle someone with his son watching. So, they were going to try to convince Mrs. O this was a bad situation and I shouldn't come, weren't they? Oh, it was *on*.

I turned, went out the door, and headed to the clearing. Mrs. O struggled to keep up with me and gasped for me to slow down. The trommel was quiet, but a quick look in the riffles showed little pieces of gravel. And the runs were wet. Neils hadn't shown me how this all worked for nothing. This sluice was running. And recently too.

"Looks like you've been running some pay dirt," I said, giving Ballcap, who had caught up to me, the stink eye.

"Just a test run," he said, stepping in front of the machine.

"And that looks like a pile of pay dirt over by the hopper," I said, pointing to the heap of gravelly dirt near the metal funnel topped with grizzly bars.

Ballcap's eyes narrowed and then a sickeningly sweet smile spread over his face as he looked to Mrs. O. "Nah, that's just soil from levelling the plant. We're still a long way from running any dirt. In fact, Frank's out looking for some parts that we're missing."

"I thought you said he didn't say where he was going?" Mrs. O said, tilting her head slightly.

"Oh yeah, I mean, he didn't say what store exactly. He didn't know where he was going to get the parts we need. Maybe he can't find them at all."

Mrs. O just gave a small nod.

I couldn't believe it. Was she falling for this?

"Well, I'm just going to wait right here until he gets back," I said, folding my arms.

Mrs. O cleared her throat. "We can stay for a bit, but I have two more appointments later this afternoon." She went to the fallen tree trunk and sat down in the shade. That reminded me I still hadn't paid Flash Gordon the burl for the bathroom fixtures.

Shifty and Ballcap made a big show of trying to fix a sluice plant that was working just fine, from what I could see. Mrs. O seemed to be dozing. I waited.

Ballcap and Shifty finally gave up and said they couldn't do any more without the missing parts, then went back to the cabin. I strained to hear the sound of a truck turning down the lane to signal my dad returning, but there was only the whine of mosquitoes and the gurgle of Cottonwood Creek.

"We had better head back, Chris," Mrs. O said, finally.

I dragged my feet back to her car and slumped in the seat. Was this it? Was it all over for my dad and me? I was so sick and tired of Dad letting me down.

"I'm staying in Dawson for a few days," she said, as the driver pulled up in front of Neils and Anna's house. "So, I'll arrange another visit with your dad before I leave. I'll let Neils know what day and time."

I had to say something. "That sluice plant *was* running. Those guys, they're . . . they were . . ."

"Lying?" Mrs. O finished for me. Then she laughed. I stared at her with my mouth hanging open.

"You knew?"

"Chris, I live in Whitehorse now, but I grew up

in Forty Mile. It's even older than Dawson and an even madder gold town. Every member of my family was mining for gold. The first word I ever said was *riffles*. I've seen more sluices in my lifetime than cars. And that sluice plant on your dad's claim was definitely running. Not to mention, I can spot a pile of pay dirt from a mile away."

I blinked. I wouldn't have guessed that in a million years.

"And you know what else I can spot from a mile away?" she said. "Someone who is stringing me a line. I get lied to all the time. Lies, exaggerations, tall tales, flimsy excuses, empty promises . . . I've heard them all. That guy wearing the hat, he couldn't even keep his story straight. And that other guy with the squinty eyes — he was using the wrong end of that spanner." She shook her head and tutted in disgust.

"I wish my dad would tell them to get lost. Please give him another chance."

Mrs. O paused for a moment. "I want to hear what he has to say before I make any decisions. I'll be in touch."

A wave of relief washed over me. We had a bit more time. But as I got out of the car and walked to the house, I had to squish down the idea bubbling up inside me that maybe my dad didn't want me to come back after all.

CHAPTER 18

FRIENDS AND ENEMIES

"I don't know what they were doing in the cabin," I told Shard the next day, between customers at the food truck, "but they looked like they'd been caught at something." I was grateful to be spending the day with Shard. Maybe she'd have a new idea of how I could fight the Filthy Rats' campaign to keep my dad and me apart. I don't know how they got around it, but the whole water licence thing didn't seem to be a problem. "What do you think they were up to?"

Shard shrugged. "Planting something to get your dad in trouble? Setting him up to lose the claim? Framing him for a crime so he goes back to jail?"

Okay, maybe I didn't want to hear her ideas. They were much worse than anything I had come up with. The worst thing I had thought of was that they were looking to steal what little money my dad had.

"You know, I can get my hands on some expired shrimp," Shard offered.

"I'll let you know," I said. "But why would you think they would want to frame him to get his claim?"

"Because it's the only thing of value he has."

I didn't answer because I knew she was right. I fell silent and bagged up some more yellowish-green popcorn. The smell was bizarre. "What is this one?"

Shard leaned over and sniffed. "Basil and lemon balm. I can't decide if it tastes like soap or pie. He calls it Presto Pesto popcorn."

"Well, it's certainly selling fast enough," I said, handing three bags out the window. "Vinnie must be making good money."

"You'd think."

"You mean he's not?"

"I mean he always seems short of cash. I don't think he's very good at managing his finances. At least that's what my mom says. He didn't even seem to have enough to buy some anti-vomit medicine."

Vinnie was so sick that morning he couldn't get out of bed, and Shard had called to see if Anna would let me help out. Fiona had come to get me. It was a tense moment when she rode up on her Ducati. Anna stiffened when she saw her out the window.

"Does she have a helmet for you? I'm not having you careening around the territory without protection."

"Yeah, she has a spare one. I'll be careful. I promise."

"She's not the most reliable person in the world," Anna muttered, turning away. Fiona didn't come in and Anna didn't go out, so I put on my jacket, said bye, and left. It was weird climbing on the Ducati again. It felt like ages since I had been on it. But this wasn't a smooth purring on the highway like our trip from the city to Dawson — this was a teeth-cracking bumpy ride on dirt roads. I was sure it couldn't be good for the bike.

"MAYDAY! MAYDAY!" I had heard Shard bellow from inside the truck when we pulled up beside it.

"You better get in there," Fiona had said, then roared off on in a cloud of dust.

I had been put right to work once I got inside. The lineup was never-ending.

"So, what's Vinnie doing with the money, then?" I asked, scooping up more stinky popcorn while I held my breath.

"I dunno. I mean, I know everything is more expensive up here, but with the lineups he has every day, he should be able to at least buy an antacid tablet or something."

I didn't know what to tell her. Maybe Vinnie was hiding his cash under his mattress. I'd heard of people doing that in the olden days when they didn't trust banks.

"Three bags of that purple popcorn," a woman at the window said. "What was it called again, Ethel?" she asked the woman behind her in line.

"Luscious Lavender," Ethel replied.

"Right, lavender. And two of the smelly lemon one. Oh, and add half a dozen Golden Nugget muffins."

"Oh, Harriet," Ethel said. "Half a dozen muffins? What about your waistline? Are you sure?"

Harriet nodded. "I have eleven loads of washing to do and I need the energy."

Harriet took her bags and left. Ethel stepped up to the window. "Two Presto Pesto popcorn," she said. Then she looked around as if to see if anyone was listening. "And half a dozen Better Than Apple Pie muffins," she whispered.

I got the order together while Shard took her money. When Ethel left, there was finally a break in the lineup.

"So, how's it going?" Shard asked me.

I didn't need to ask *How's what going?* because Shard and I think the same. She meant the water licence plan to keep the Filthy Rats from mining.

"That sluice was running, but I don't know how. It's too soon for them to have gotten a permit. I guess the plan didn't work after all."

"You know, Vinnie has some laxatives in his medicine cabinet," she said, "if you need me to bake some *special* brownies."

"I'll keep that in mind," I said. I wasn't above trying *anything* to get them away from my dad.

We worked until about five o'clock. By then all the smelly popcorn was sold out and most of the muffins were gone too.

"Do you need me again tomorrow?" I asked Shard, as Fiona pulled up on the Ducati.

"No. Fiona's sister said she would look after their mom for the day so Fiona can come. We can video chat later if you need to brainstorm more ideas." Shard handed me a container of day-old muffins and a bag of popcorn. I didn't ask what flavour it was. "This is the best I can do for payment."

I looked at the bag of popcorn. "Thanks. I'll let Anna have this with her tea," I said, giving it a sniff. I snapped on the helmet, climbed on the Ducati, and waved goodbye.

If it were possible, the roads were even bumpier

on the trip back. It didn't help that we were following a pickup truck that was full of scrap and kicking up a choking amount of dust. It looked like it was heading to Flash Gordon's junkyard. I heard a clunk as it went over a particularly large pothole.

All of a sudden the Ducati tilted and swerved. I grabbed on tighter to the back of Fiona's jacket, trying to keep from falling off the bike. Fiona seemed to hunch over but we kept on going. The pickup turned onto the lane for the junkyard.

When we reached Anna and Neils's house, Fiona turned off the engine and slumped over, holding her right arm.

"Are you okay?" I asked. I couldn't see what had happened but there was blood on her jacket, above the elbow.

"I think I should get the bleeding to stop before I head home," she admitted. Then she looked up at the front door where Anna was standing, arms crossed.

"On second thought, I think I can make it back like this," Fiona said to me.

I looked over at Anna.

"Don't just sit there," she said to Fiona. "Get inside."

"It's just a scrape," Fiona said, straightening up.

Anna stomped down the wooden steps of the

front porch and practically yanked Fiona off her bike. "You never were very sensible," Anna huffed.

Fiona scowled but allowed herself to be led inside.

I followed behind. This was going to be *very* interesting.

Anna pulled out a chair from the kitchen table for Fiona to sit on and went to the cupboard above the fridge for her first-aid supplies. Fiona held on to her arm and said nothing.

"You have to let me see," Anna said, coming over to her and trying to pull Fiona's hand away from her arm.

"Only if you want blood spraying all across your floor," Fiona said.

"Oh, stop exaggerating. Show me the cut."

Fiona stood up. "I think the bleeding's stopped now. I'll just head home and wrap it up."

"Sit down, Fi." Anna folded her arms. "I took you down once before, and I'm not afraid to do it again."

Fiona glanced over at me. I quickly closed my gaping mouth and looked out the window as if I was fascinated with what the garden gnomes were doing.

"Yeah, you sure showed your true colours that day," Fiona said, almost hissing.

"You deserved everything you got," Anna said, her eyes narrowing. "Now give me that arm."

Fiona finally sat down again and let go of her sleeve. I could see her jacket was ripped in a smooth straight line and blood was seeping through the slit.

"Take your jacket off," Anna told her, soaking a gauze pad in alcohol. Fiona pulled it off.

"Not a very sturdy jacket," Anna said. "Looks like a knock-off."

"Nothing would have stopped that flying piece of metal. No matter what kind of jacket or where it came from."

"You drive too fast."

"You can't keep your mouth shut."

It was suddenly very awkward to be sitting in the room with them. I wondered if I could slip out unnoticed.

Anna came at Fiona with the alcohol-soaked gauze.

"That's going to sting," Fiona said, trying to pull her arm away.

"Uh-huh."

Fiona pressed her lips together and looked away. Anna grinned.

"Tsssssss," Fiona said.

After cleaning the wound, Anna covered it with dry gauze and wrapped it in a bandage.

"That should get you home," she said.

"Thanks," Fiona mumbled. She got up and nodded toward me. "Thanks for helping today, Chris. It's nice to be able to count on people."

I looked at Anna — her face had gone pale.

"Sure. No problem," I said. "Hope Vinnie's feeling better."

Fiona gave a two-finger salute with her left hand and pushed the front door open violently, letting it slam behind her. Then I heard the Ducati's engine roar to life and the tires crunch their way down the gravel lane.

Anna muttered to herself as she cleaned up and didn't even hear Neils come in.

"Was that Fi I saw driving away?" he asked.

Anna turned around, her eyes narrowed.

"Uh, never mind. I didn't see anything. Or anyone," he said. Neils looked at me questioningly as Anna went to put the first-aid box away. I shrugged. I had no idea what was going on, but I understood one thing: Fiona and Anna had a history. And whatever had happened between them, it hadn't ended well.

"You want to help me feed the dogs?" Neils asked.

I nodded and jumped up. Anna was still scowling, and I was more than happy to get out of the house for a while.

Neils mixed up the dog stew and I helped him ladle it into their bowls. I fed Bullet first. He thanked me with a nudge that almost knocked me over.

By the time we fed the last of the dogs, the first ones were finished. This time Bullet licked my ear to say thanks. Lately Neils had been running the dogs really early in the morning. Maybe tomorrow I would drag myself out of bed in time to join him. "So, what's the deal with Anna and Fiona?" I dared to ask, as we walked back to the house.

Neils rubbed his chin. "Well, it's still a pretty sore subject." He looked around as if he were worried Anna was hiding behind a tree or something. "And I don't know if I should say anything, but Anna turned Fiona in to the Mounties."

"For what?"

"Theft."

Fiona, a thief? "What did she steal?"

"That high-end motorcycle."

"The Ducati?!"

Neils shrugged. "Well, that's what everyone thought. One day she's riding some patched-together piece of junk, and then the next day she's on that Italian superbike."

"That doesn't mean she stole it."

"No, but one just like it had been stolen in Whitehorse the week before."

"Could just be a coincidence!" I don't know why I felt so strongly about sticking up for Fiona. After all, she was pretty prickly. But she *did* drop everything and offer to drive me up here to Dawson so I could get my granddad's claim back. And she even registered it for me before someone else could snatch it away from us again. A thief would have taken it for herself.

"So, why was it Anna who turned her in?" I asked.

"Anna was protecting the club. Said the RCMP was on their case enough as it was, and they didn't want criminals for members."

"What club?"

"The Ladyhawks."

I almost felt a little dizzy. I remembered the leather jacket Fiona let me wear on the ride north and the dark shape where a patch had been. Fiona had told me she ripped it off and burned it when her club betrayed her. "You mean the motorcycle club? Anna was a biker?"

Neils broke out in a huge grin. "Don't let that sweet little blond who cooks like a dream fool you," he said. "She was a wild child in her day." Then he winked. "That's why I married her."

I tried to think about Anna and Fiona together in a biker club. I just couldn't see it.

"So, what happened? Did Fiona go to jail?"

"Fiona went to the RCMP detachment for questioning. She was released after hours and hours. She was never charged. She came looking for Anna and took a swing at her when she found her." Neils stopped walking and put his hands in his pockets. "Anna is a black belt in aikido, you know. She took Fi down in fifteen seconds. I was at my mine that day." He started walking again, shaking his head. "I'm sorry I missed it. Anyway, that was the last time they spoke. Until today."

We were back at the house, and Neils put a finger to his lips to remind me not to say anything. As if. Now that I knew Anna was a black belt, I was going to be *very* careful around her.

CHAPTER 19

STRANGER DANGER

I waited impatiently on the front steps of the house for Mrs. Olsen. She had promised she would be back today to take me for another visit. I hoped that even though my dad didn't show at the last visit, she had spoken to him like she planned and he had explained everything. Maybe it had gone so well that this was the last time I'd have to have supervision.

Finally a car came crunching up the laneway, but the lady getting out wasn't Mrs. O. This person was taller, slimmer and had short, spiky grey hair. I got a bad feeling.

"You must be Christopher," she said, marching up to me.

"Chris," I corrected her.

"Well, Christopher. I'm Mrs. Tarantella, your new caseworker."

"Where is Mrs. Olsen?"

Mrs. New CPS pursed her lips and folded her arms. "You should say, 'Nice to meet you, Mrs. Tarantella' first."

I scowled. Really? I was getting lectured on my manners by a stranger? I folded my arms too. It was a standoff. She gave in first with an exasperated sigh.

"Where are . . ." She swiped her phone screen. ". . . Neils and Anna Amundson?"

"Inside."

She brushed past me and knocked on the screen. Anna came to the door.

"Hello, I'm Mrs. Tarantella from CPS."

Anna craned her neck to look over her shoulder. "Where's Mrs. Olsen?"

Mrs. Tarantula, or whatever her name was, gave another big sigh and shot me a dirty look. I noticed she didn't lecture Anna on not greeting her first, though.

"She's had to have her leg bone reset in surgery. She's not going anywhere for a while."

"Oh, so you're her temporary replacement," Anna said. "Well, Chris is ready for you, as you can see."

I wasn't sure about going over to see my dad with this lady — even just driving to the next claim would feel like a long car ride.

"I need to speak to you and Neils first."

"Okay, come in." Anna held the screen open for her. I followed her in.

"I need to speak to the Amundsons in private, Christopher," she said, blocking my way.

Anna gave me an *I'm sorry* smile, so I turned around and went back outside. This had better be quick — it was cutting into my visit time. I wondered what she had to say to them. Maybe she was wanting to lighten her caseload and was ready to reunite me with my dad? I crept around the house and crouched under the open living-room window to listen in.

"There are . . . irregularities . . . in your application process. Irregularities that I cannot overlook," I heard Mrs. T say.

This didn't sound like things were moving forward with my case.

"No, no, no." I heard Neils say. "It was all done and settled properly. We're foster parents and Chris is staying with us."

"Irregularities that can't be overlooked," Mrs. Tarantella repeated. "Mrs. Olsen seemed to have skipped several steps in approving you both as foster parents. Your case is being reviewed."

"And what does that mean?" Neils asked.

"If we can't resolve the discrepancies, well, we will have to revoke your status as foster parents."

"Revoke? What do you mean 'revoke'? We were approved."

"Not according to our records."

"And what will happen to Chris?" Anna asked.

Yes, what will happen to me? I couldn't move, couldn't breath. *Please say that I would go back with my dad,* I prayed.

"He will be placed with another, certified, foster family."

"Here in Dawson?"

"No, probably back in Whitehorse. We have several acceptable families there."

"You can't possibly do this to him now. To us now," Anna said. "He is just settling in."

"Children are resilient. He'll be fine."

"No, he WON'T be fine. He needs to be here, with us," Neils said.

"And near his father," Anna added.

"Ah yes," Mrs. Tarantella said, "his father. Seems he has not met any of the requirements we set for him in order to regain guardianship of his son."

I slumped to the ground. I felt like I was going to black out.

"He just needs a little more time," Anna said.

"I am not Francis Dearing's caseworker. I am Chris's. And if his father is incapable of looking after him, then we need to move on."

I couldn't listen anymore. I jumped up and ran. I would rather face a full-sized moose than stay there a minute longer. Without planning it, I ended up at the dog yard. Bullet seemed happy to see me, and I knelt down and buried my face in his coat.

That's where Neils found me a while later, after I'd heard my caseworker's car crunch back down the lane.

"Figured you'd be here," he said, giving Bullet a quick pat. "I take it you heard?"

I stood up. "I'm not going. I'll run away first."

Neils put his hands up, palms out. "Now hold on there. No one is going anywhere."

"I heard what she said. She wants to send me to Whitehorse."

"She said she was looking into it. Nothing is going to happen right away. Besides, your dad is going to show them he is able to take care of you before anything happens."

I looked to the ground where Bullet's paws had worn away the plants, leaving only dirt. I desperately wanted to believe my dad was getting his act together, but if I was really honest, he had let me down before. He meant well, but he was so easily swayed by people. Especially bad people. Like the Filthy Rats. If I was going to have any chance at all, I was going to have to get rid of them. That is, if I wasn't shipped five hundred kilometres away to Whitehorse first.

"So, I can't visit my dad today?" I asked.

Neils threw his shoulders back. "Until someone tells me differently, I can still supervise your visits. Let's go."

When we pulled up to the cabin, all was quiet. I got out first, ran to the door, and pushed it open. Inside was a total mess. Dirty dishes were piled in the small basin and all over the wooden table. Garbage littered the counter and floor. The bedsheets were half off the mattress and clothes were everywhere. I checked to make sure Granddad's artifacts weren't broken, but they weren't in the rafters. Dad must have moved them. I went out to the bathhouse, knowing what I'd find. Sure enough, no work had been done since the last time I was there. Neils said nothing as he looked over my shoulder.

We could hear the sluice plant as we approached. When we got there, it was only Shifty and Ballcap. And they did *not* look happy to see us.

"So, you got your plant up and working?" Neils said, casually walking over to the sluice with his hands in his pockets.

"Yeah," Shifty said.

"Looks like rich pay dirt. Getting a good cleanup?"

"Doing okay."

"How'd you get your water licence so fast?"

Ballcap glared. "Turns out we don't need one if we top up our daily limit with water in a reservoir. Luckily our buddy in town let us in on that little detail," Ballcap said.

"Yeah, but we had to pay $300 for a holding tank, a hose and a pump," Shifty grumbled.

Neils shrugged. "Just following the rules."

Shifty and Ballcap both shot Neils dirty looks.

"Where's my dad?" I asked.

"Uh, he's in town. Getting supplies."

In town? Did he leave because we were later than planned? Not to mention that was the last place he should be. He would have to walk past at least five or six bars to get to the General Store. I felt defeated.

"Neils? Can we go home?"

Neils turned around. "Don't you want to wait for your dad?"

"Nah. I'll catch him some other time," I said.

Neils's eyes narrowed, but he began walking anyway. "You guys take care now," he said over his shoulder. Shifty and Ballcap watched us leave.

We got in the truck and headed down the lane. The only good thing about today was that

Mrs. T had been too busy trying to strip Neils and Anna of their foster-parent status to come for the check-in.

"Instead of going straight home," I said, "would you mind if we went into Dawson? I have, um, an errand to run."

"You want to find your dad, heh?"

I nodded.

"Chris, we're in enough hot water with CPS already. We don't want to do anything that will jeopardize our situation with you. I'm pretty sure Mrs. Tarantella won't look kindly on me dragging you around Dawson to look for your dad."

"I need to help him, Neils. If I don't, and Mrs. Tarantella finds him first, well." I gulped. "I'm doomed. I need to talk to him."

Neils sighed really long and hard. "I have a few words I'd like to say to him myself," he muttered.

He didn't say much else to me as we drove into town. "Just let me off on the corner here," I said.

"Nope," Neils said. "I'm not letting you go into the bars. For sure that wouldn't fly with CPS. Besides, you're too young, and they can be kind of rough."

I didn't argue. I had dragged my dad out of enough bars back in the city to know that was true.

"Let's try the Westminster Hotel first," I said. "It looks like the kind of place he used to like."

We parked along Third Avenue and headed down the boardwalk. Inside the hotel we saw the entrance to the bar. It didn't make me feel any better to learn it was called the Pit.

"You wait out here," Neils said, then he went in.

He came out shaking his head. It was the same with Bombay Peggy's, the Sluice Box Lounge and Diamond Tooth Gerties. Neils couldn't find him anywhere.

"He must have already gone home," Neils said. "Come on. While we're here, I need to get some gear at the Trading Post."

I reluctantly walked back over to the truck and scanned every bit of the boardwalk for my dad as Neils drove around to Front Street.

I loved going into the Trading Post. Sure, it had mining, fishing and camping gear, but it also had lots of old stuff. There were shelves holding lanterns, tins and books, and in the glass cases near the cash register were coins, buckles, small blades and portable gold scales.

While Neils talked to Ian about the best lures for the fishing trip he was planning with Leo, I rummaged around the old stuff. I liked seeing how they made things work before computer chips and electronics. I was amazed that a miner's lamp just like the one Shard and I had found was worth over a hundred dollars. Of course, mine was worth more to me because my granddad had probably used it.

"We're off, Chris," Neils said, paying for his lures and a new reel for his rod. I followed him out, giving one more look up and down the street before I climbed in the truck. Where was he?

That night I woke up from a nightmare where I was sliding down a muddy pit on a mine site. The bottom was just a black hole and the sides were slick and wet. There was nothing to grab to stop my fall. I sat bolt upright in bed, sweat dripping down my back, heart pounding, mouth dry. I didn't want to analyze what it meant . . . I think I knew anyway. I went to the window and opened the blind. Outside was a murky dusk, and I thought I could just make out the shapes of the trees on our claim. Would I get this close only to lose it all?

CHAPTER 20

THE COLOUR OF INNOCENCE

The next day everything was still; there wasn't so much as a breeze. Through my open window I could even hear the sluice plant running on the Dearing claim. The sound put me on edge. It should have made me happy, because it meant pay dirt was being run, but I knew my dad was probably sleeping off his trip into town while the Filthy Rats robbed him.

I had my granddad's file open on my bed. I kept reading it over and over trying to find a detail that would prove my granddad didn't do it. It was like each time I read the newspaper reports, I hoped for a different ending — one where my grandfather wasn't a thief who had stolen gold because there wasn't any on the claim.

"You up for a run to Flash Gordon's?" Neils asked, poking his head in my room. "We need a new belt for the dryer."

"You bet," I said, closing the file and sticking it back under my socks in my drawer. I don't really know why I was hiding it; I just didn't like it out in the open, as if leaving it there was airing all our dirty laundry.

When we got to the junkyard, I realized I didn't have any popcorn to bribe Lucy. I looked over at Neils. He had a bead of sweat on his forehead. We both sat in the parking lot for a moment before trying to get out of the truck. It was quiet outside. Too quiet. I had hoped there would be other cars there so Lucy might be distracted, but the parking lot was empty.

Neils cleared his throat. "Here, I grabbed this from the cupboard. Don't tell Anna."

He passed me a handful of purple popcorn. I felt better being armed for battle. We gave each other a nod and bravely flung the truck doors open. Although we didn't say anything, I noticed we were both trying to step on the small weeds poking through the gravel because it made less noise. We were almost to the dredge when we heard it: the angry flapping of large wings. Neils panicked and threw his handful of popcorn wildly in the air, not even in the direction of Lucy. I looked back. She was not impressed. She stopped with her wings open, staring at Neils's back. I swear, if she could, she would have put her wings on her hips and shaken her head in disgust.

We made it through the door, and Neils closed it behind us, probably harder than he meant to. Gordon came down the stairs at the sound.

"You seem to be in a bit of hurry," he said to Neils, grinning.

"I, uh, the wind must have caught the door," Neils said.

Gordon winked at me.

"What are you looking for today?" he asked Neils.

"I need a new belt for our dryer."

Gordon rubbed his chin. "I don't have any new ones, but you can see if any will fit from the ones in the yard. They're around back."

Neils gave a glance over his shoulder toward the door.

"I'm sure Lucy won't follow you back there. She's afraid of toilets."

"Right," Neils said, and headed out the door, but not without looking left and right first.

"Wanna give me a hand?" Gordon asked.

"Sure. With what?"

"I promised the Dawson archives some of my father's records and ledgers. I'm just trying to gather it all up."

I followed Gordon back upstairs and into a

room stuffed full of boxes. A truck rumbled by on the road.

"Was that thunder?" he asked, in a panic. "Did you hear thunder?"

"No. It was just a truck."

"Oh," Flash Gordon said, his hands trembling slightly.

"So, what did your dad do?" I asked, trying to distract him.

"He was a gold buyer in Dawson. Worked with the dredge companies."

"Really? I wonder if he knew my granddad. He worked on one of the dredges."

"What was his name?"

I gulped a little. Maybe I shouldn't have said anything.

"Wallace Dearing," I said, hoping the name didn't mean anything to him.

Gordon looked up in surprise.

"You're Wally's grandson? Neils never said you were a Dearing!"

I smiled weakly.

"My dad always felt bad about what happened to him," Gordon said.

"What do you mean?"

"You know, good gold buyers knew their gold. They could even tell which creek it came from just by looking at it."

"How?"

"By the colour."

"Isn't it all yellow?"

Gordon shook his head. "Not really. There is no such thing as finding pure gold — it always has some other metal in it. Now, the gold from Bonanza Creek — the dredge's gold — has about ten percent silver in it, so it's a lighter yellow. Up Forty Mile way, there is more copper in the gold, so it's a deeper reddish colour."

"What does that have to do with my granddad?"

Gordon stopped digging in the boxes and looked right at me. "My dad said there was no way the gold Wally Dearing tried to sell him was Bonanza Creek gold. No way it was from the dredge. He said it was the colour of an Irish maiden's hair. It was Forty Mile gold."

"Cottonwood Creek starts near Forty Mile," I said. "So, Granddad was telling the truth — he didn't steal it from the dredge. It came from the claim."

I was shaking I was so excited. Maybe I wasn't from a family of losers after all.

"Wait, if he knew it wasn't stolen, then why didn't your dad say something?" I asked.

"Because he left on his rounds right after your granddad came to see him. They hadn't finished the deal because Wally said he wanted to clean up his gold a bit before selling it. You get a better price that way. So, they had agreed to meet again when my dad got back. Part of Dad's job was to visit some of the more remote camps on his way down to Whitehorse to ship the gold out."

"He could have said something when he got back," I said bitterly.

"Don't forget there was no highway back then. He went by horse on the way down and then took the Klondike paddle steamer back up the Yukon River. Took him more than four weeks. By the time he got back, Wally had left Dawson."

I let that sink in. There was proof my granddad wasn't a thief, but it came too late to save him.

"Where'd he go?"

Gordon shrugged. "No one really knew. But about a dozen summers later he showed up back in Dawson with a new young wife — your grandma Emma — and enough money to buy a new claim."

I thought back over the files Leo had given me. I remembered seeing that the company had eventually dropped the charges. Maybe they had figured out he wasn't guilty.

"But what about the claim on Cottonwood Creek?"

Gordon shook his head. "The courts had awarded it back to the previous owners. Something about it not being a legal sale."

I heard Neils come back inside, calling for me.

"Thanks, Gordon," I said, my voice cracking. "Even if no one else believes it, you've cleared my granddad's name for me."

I couldn't wait to tell my dad. When we got back to Neils's place, I snuck across the creek and over to the Dearing claim to tell him the news.

I was too late.

CHAPTER 21

WOLVES, COYOTES AND BEARS, OH MY!

As I got to the claim, I recognized the car parked in front of the cabin. It belonged to Mrs. Tarantella. And based on the conversation coming from inside, things were going downhill — fast.

"Sanitary, Mr. Dearing," I heard her say. "That means a bathroom with no dirt, no insects, no mould and no raccoons. So that is a big fat X on that requirement. Sleeping arrangements. He needs a proper, *clean* bed with some privacy. And no, your shirts hanging up to dry do not count as a screen."

"It's just a matter of . . ." my dad started to say.

"No, it's not just a matter of. You were given a deadline, Mr. Dearing. A deadline to have this all in place. You were also supposed to register with the local public health nurse for addiction counselling. Have you done that?"

I could hear my dad mumbling.

"I've heard enough. Mrs. Olsen has given you more than enough time. I'm afraid that time is up. I am putting in a recommendation to have Christopher remain in foster care and have him relocated to Whitehorse, where I can keep a better eye on him. Things have been way too lax around here. Well, that's going to end."

"Relocated?" my dad said, much louder. "What's wrong with where he is?"

"The Amundsons were not properly certified. He will be placed with one of our more reliable families for his own good."

My dad went silent. I could feel the blood drain from my face. She was really going to do it. She was going to rip me away from my dad and Neils and Anna and take me to Whitehorse where I would probably be forgotten and never get back. I ran through the bush back to the house, barely feeling the thistles rip at my skin. When I got back, Anna was outside.

"There you are. Where did you go? Mrs. Tarantella is coming," she said, "and the last thing I need is for her to think that I don't know where you are."

I had to try to catch my breath. "I'm not going in there," I panted.

"Chris . . ." Anna started.

I held up a hand. "No. She wants to take me away. Away from you and Neils. Away from the claim. Away from my dad. I'm not going to let her do that. I'll run away first."

Anna looked stricken. "Run away? Not only will that not work, but it's dangerous. Running away in the city might mean a cold night in an alley with rats, but here it means being stalked by wolves, coyotes or bears while battling hypothermia. Not to mention if you accidentally wander onto someone's claim and they think you are a thief, you could be attacked by guard dogs, security or even angry owners."

"I don't care. I'm not going to be sent away."

"Ever hear the saying that the Mounties always get their man? That's no joke. The RCMP officers can track down anyone up here."

"I am *not* going to Whitehorse," I said.

"No. But you *are* coming into the house," she said, putting a hand on my shoulder and pushing me to the house. "I don't need her thinking you run wild here and we aren't responsible. Maybe if she sees how committed we are and how well you are doing here, we can smooth things over."

When Mrs. Tarantella arrived, I sat at the dining-room table with Anna and Neils. I had to grit my teeth as I listened to the list of things Mrs. T was putting in her report. My dad didn't do this. My dad didn't do that. Neils didn't attend some meeting. Anna didn't fill out some paperwork. I wasn't making friends. My dad wasn't making money. And the whole time I was plotting how to run away before she could take me away. I wasn't scared — I'd done it before when Family Services was on my tail in the city. Well, maybe I was a little scared. Anna kept talking about bears, wolves and freezing to death.

"Pack bear spray," I muttered to myself.

"What was that, Christopher?" Mrs. Tarantella asked, looking annoyed. "Do you have something you want to share?"

I stared back at her. Who knew that Mrs. Olsen would someday look like a friendly ally? My mom used to say, "Be grateful for what you have, because it can always be worse." Boy, was she right. Mrs. Tarantella was fifty times worse than Mrs. Olsen.

I wanted to swear or something. Something to shock her. But then I saw Anna giving me that *don't you dare* look.

"No. Nothing to share," I said.

Mrs. Tarantella straightened her pile of forms by banging the edges on the table, then stuffed them into her briefcase. "I'll have this all sorted out in a few days." She got up. Anna tried to reason with her and show how good this was for all of us. Neils even threatened to go over her head. None of it made any difference. Mrs. Tarantella just pursed her lips tighter and walked out.

After she left, I stomped to my room and began packing. Then I thought I had better let Shard know. She'd freak out if I just left without telling her. Maybe I could hide out in Vinnie's truck?

I sent the email and waited. I hate waiting. Where was she? Why did everyone abandon me when I needed them most?

There was a soft knock on my door. Neils poked his head in. "Can I come in?"

I nodded. Neils sat on the black desk chair that didn't look like it could hold him. "Anna mentioned you have some plans."

I said nothing, tired of explaining.

"She said you were pretty determined, and I can't say that I blame you. But I'm just asking you to wait a bit."

"Mrs. T could come back tomorrow and drag me away. No way am I taking that chance!"

Neils held up a hand. "Hold on there. Mrs. Tarantella said it would take a couple of days."

"She's probably lying."

"But I'm not. And I need you to give us some time to work this out."

"Work it out how?"

"I'm putting in a call to Mrs. Tarantella. We've

put in the new paperwork as foster parents and I know we can reason with her. Convince her to just delay until we're officially approved. Will you promise me to stay put for a bit? Give Anna and me a chance to make this right."

My shoulders drooped. If I was honest with myself, I didn't want to go on the run again. It was exhausting.

"Okay."

Neils gave me a slap on the shoulder and got up to leave. "Good. So, would you like to help me run the dogs?"

Even Bullet couldn't cheer me up today, so I told Neils I didn't feel like it. I sat at the computer and started playing Wizarding World instead. It was just as well, because the sky started to get so dark that I had to turn on my desk light. Then I saw a flash. Lightning. I counted. "One one-thousand, two one-thousand, three one-thousand." I got to twelve before I heard a low, distant rumble of thunder. Four kilometres away. Another flash. "One one-thousand, two one-thousand . . ." That one was three kilometres away. The time between the flashes and rumbles kept getting shorter. The storm was getting closer. I tried to concentrate on the game but I shuddered. I didn't mind storms when I was safe inside, so I was glad I hadn't gone with Neils. He wasn't afraid of storms, but I wouldn't want to be out in the woods when lightning hit close by.

Like that one!

The flash and the rumble were almost at the same time. You could feel the vibration in the ground as the air boomed. I went out to the kitchen to find Anna.

"That was close," she said, when she saw me. She looked out the window. "I hope Neils gets back soon."

The sky flashed again. This time it looked almost purple. The crack of thunder was not even a one one-thousand after it. The ground trembled again. We both spun around as Neils burst through the door.

"Woowee! That one almost fried my whiskers," he said, his hair standing on end. "Glad we weren't too far away. Let me tell you, Bullet and the team were flying on the way back. I think they wanted to be tucked safe inside their houses too."

"I'm glad you're back before the rain starts," Anna said. "You'd be drenched through."

"I wish it were raining," Neils said. "Lightning without water is something I fear. I always think disaster is just around the corner."

As if on cue, the phone rang. Anna answered it, but after a moment she handed it to Neils without a word. "I'll be right there," he said.

He pressed *End* and looked at Anna. "Fire."

Like most men in Dawson, Neils was a volunteer firefighter.

Anna paled. "Where?"

"The junkyard. I've got to go."

The junkyard? Flash Gordon's place was on fire? I sure hoped Gordon had some decent luck and the fire was in one of the piles of fence posts or old oil tanks and not the dredge, which was made completely of tinder-dry, one-hundred-year-old wood.

I watched from the porch as Neils took off down the lane. As the dust settled I heard the *whoop, whoop, whoop* of a helicopter heading to the scene. I looked up as it flew over the house, carrying a massive bucket on the end of a wire. It flew north toward the junkyard. Anna joined me on the porch, and we stood staring at the wisps of grey smoke rising and twisting in the air above the trees in the distance. The smoke seemed to be getting thicker and thicker. Was it going to spread to the woods? The flashes and rumbling continued but were finally moving farther away.

"I can't stand it," Anna said. "Let's head over to help. There must be something we can do."

I grabbed my jacket and we jumped in the car. The road near the junkyard was choked with trucks and cars. We parked along Hunker Creek

Road so we wouldn't get in the way of the volunteer firefighters. We made our way down the lane slowly, dodging people, trucks and hoses.

When we got close enough to see, the flames were out, but the back half of the dredge was completely gone. The yard looked like a tornado had torn through. All the piles Gordon had so carefully sorted had been ripped apart by firefighters checking for smouldering embers.

Some firefighters still worked to make sure the fire was completely out. Others put up yellow caution tape all around the dredge. The crew and helpers started thinning out; pickups and cars began leaving.

I looked around and finally saw Gordon under a tree, stroking Lucy's head and watching the last wisps of smoke rise from what was left of his home. He was smiling. *Smiling*. Now, I've seen people crack up before. After his wife died, old man Cheevers in Sunnyview Terrace found a mouse living under his sink and used to set a place for it at the table. He even carved a bed for it out of a plastic vitamin bottle so it could sleep beside him. And Ms. Nabeeb in 2F put her houseplants out in the hall overnight because she thought they could read her mind while she slept. Now Flash Gordon was smiling as he looked at the smouldering ruin of his house. I guess shock does strange things to people. I would have to be careful with what I said to him. I didn't want him to snap and let Lucy attack me. I hadn't remembered to bring any popcorn.

"Hey there, Gordon. Can I get you anything?" I asked him.

He looked at me with a big toothy grin. "Nah. I'm good." Lucy *gleeped* in agreement.

"Um, good?" I asked. "Are you sure?"

He nodded, still grinning.

"You seem awfully happy for a guy who just lost his home," I blurted out. So much for being careful with what I said.

"This is my lucky day."

"Lucky? To have your house burn down?"

Gordon shook his head. "Good luck or bad luck all depends on how you look at something. And you are looking at this all wrong. Don't you see? The lightning struck the dredge and not me. This is the first time I wasn't the target. My unlucky streak is over!"

With that, he strolled off like he didn't have a care in the world. I wondered if that were possible, what he said about luck changing. Could that really happen? Could you be a target for terrible things one day, and then disaster forgets you and finds a new victim the next? Boy, I sure hoped so. Maybe then *my* unlucky streak would end too.

CHAPTER 22

EVERYONE LIKES CHRIS

The day after the fire we got word that Dawsonites were mounting a silent auction to raise money for Flash Gordon. Anna bid on some crayon drawings by Mrs. Haney's kids, which she had taken right off her fridge and framed. Neils was in a heated bidding battle for a load of gravel put up by Donaldson's Construction Company. If I had any money, I think I would have bid on the jar of bearberry jam. Shard told me bearberries got their name because they smell a bit like wet, stinky bear. That couldn't be true, could it? Would people really make jam out of that?

I was really glad everyone was trying to help Flash Gordon, but at the same time I had my own looming problem. Mrs. T could be coming back at any moment to drag me away to Whitehorse. Neils had said to give him time to work it out, but with him busy fighting fires and participating in auctions . . . it seemed like I was way down the list again. My dad didn't seem to be able to rescue me, Neils and Anna were distracted, Mrs. Olsen was missing in action and Mrs. T was trying to take me away from everyone and everything I knew. So far, the most reliable people in my life were an ex-biker bar owner, a friend who lived thousands of kilometres away most of the year and the Muffin Man.

The next day Neils and I went into town to pick up more popcorn to battle the ants and some new rubber boots at the Trading Post.

"Have you heard from Mrs. T?" I asked, as we bumped along.

"I got an email saying she would call this afternoon. She's aware of our position and is looking into it."

Looking into it. What did that mean, exactly? Would she let things stay as they were for now and not move me to Whitehorse?

The Trading Post was busy, so I nosed around while Neils tried to find his size in the stack of boxes at the end of a narrow aisle full of customers. I gravitated to the antiques again. I liked thinking of the person who might have used the things a hundred years ago. Like the miner's lamp that was still sitting on the shelf. I looked in the locked cabinet against the far wall. This was where the store owner, Ian, kept what he called "oddities." The labels identified a human tooth with a diamond embedded in it, a taxidermied three-headed chick, a plaster cast of what was supposed to be a sasquatch footprint and a Mason jar with a human toe in it. My blood ran cold. There was no mistaking that ugly toe.

Wait a minute! I ran back to the lamp. It not only looked like the one we dug up, it *was* the one we dug up. There was that same small crack in the glass. I went to the counter where Ian was handing a lady her bag.

"Excuse me," I said.

"Heya, Chris. What can I get you?"

"Um, that Mason jar in the cabinet over there, the one with the toe in it. Where did you get it?"

Ian craned his neck to look over my shoulder at the cabinet.

"Oh yeah. Fellow brought it in a few days ago with a couple of other things."

I did a quick calculation in my head. That would be right around when I saw the Filthy Rats alone in the cabin, looking guilty.

"What other things?" I asked. "One wouldn't be that miner's lamp on the shelf, would it?"

"Yeah," Ian said slowly, his eyebrows knitting together. "And some gold scales. Why?"

"Which gold scales?"

Ian pointed to a set of scales in the glass-topped case beside the cash register. They were exactly like the ones I had found in the garden, only without the wooden box with *WD* carved into it.

"Who brought it in?"

"Why do you want to know?"

"Those were my granddad's things. I found them on his claim and in his cabin."

Ian's eyes narrowed. "So, you're saying you think they're stolen? That's a serious accusation to make."

"I know. But when I checked on them a couple of days ago, they weren't there."

"That doesn't necessarily mean these are the same ones. Is there anyone who can corroborate this?"

I wanted to explain to Ian how the image of that toe was seared into my brain, but that wasn't really proof. Then I remembered: "Vinnie! Vinnie and Shard saw them when we dug them up."

Ian walked over to the two cases and removed the jar with the toe and the gold scales.

"That miner's lamp over there too," I said.

"I'll look into this," he said, putting the items behind the counter. I hoped he wasn't mad at me for mentioning it. What if I was wrong? I wanted to ask him what he was going to do, but then customers, including Neils, came up to pay for their items. We left without me getting a chance to ask.

Our next stop was Vinnie's food truck. Perfect. I could make sure Vinnie and Shard would back me up if Ian asked them about the lamp and the scales. Vinnie had a huge lineup and no help, so I had to wait until he was between customers.

"Where are Fiona and Shard?"

"Fiona went to Whitehorse for me. I needed a new burner for my popcorn kettle and there's none in Dawson. She should be back this evening. And Shard has a bad headache. She's sleeping back at the apartment."

Shoot. Shard would remember everything exactly. Vinnie? That was a little murkier.

"So, I was wondering something. Do you remember that lamp we found when we were digging up the garden on the Dearing claim?"

"Sure, I remember the lamp. Copper, wasn't it?" he said.

"No, brass."

"And a tin cup . . .?"

"Small gold scales."

"Right. Right. Um, what was it you wanted with them again?"

"If Ian from the Trading Post asks you to identify them, could you?"

"Sure. Sure. Here, have some popcorn."

I wasn't so sure, though. He didn't seem that solid on the facts. I wished Shard were here.

Popcorn in hand, Neils and I climbed in the truck to head back to the house. I kicked myself for not looking for survival gear at the Trading Post in case I was on the run again in a couple of days.

I wondered if I should go to the RCMP about the items from the claim, but the way Ian reacted, I got the impression a false accusation might land *me* in more trouble than the Filthy Rats. I didn't know what to do. It was eating me up that the Filthy Rats stole my granddad's things and were selling them. I hoped that maybe I'd come up with a plan while I slept that night.

* * *

The next morning something was up with Anna. She was all business. As soon as Neils and I walked in the door from feeding the dogs, she pulled him into their bedroom for a private talk. I could hear muffled voices, but I couldn't tell what was going on. They came back out of the room, and now Neils was all serious too. He left in his truck, and when he came back about an hour and a half later, he had a passenger: Shard.

"What's going on?" I asked. Don't get me wrong, I was thrilled to see Shard, but I knew something was brewing if Neils had made a special trip into town just to get her. No doubt about it — there was about to be some bad news.

"Mrs. Tarantella called," Anna said. "She's, um, coming to Dawson to talk to us in person."

Now it all made sense. They brought Shard here to make sure I didn't bolt. Boy, they didn't know Shard at all. After all, she came along when I ran away to Dawson in the first place.

Inside I was seething, but I didn't want Neils and Anna to see that.

"Wanna meet Bullet?" I asked Shard, hoping she'd get the hint that I wanted to talk. In private.

"You and your dogs," she said, but nodded.

I saw Neils and Anna exchange glances. "We won't be long," I said, reassuring them that I wasn't going on the run. Yet.

Shard and I walked to the dog yard. "So, what are we going to do?" she asked.

"I can't give up on my dad now," I said. "I know he can straighten up. I know there's gold on the claim. We just need a chance to prove it. Mrs. Olsen was willing to work with us, but this Mrs. T is ruining everything. Once she gets back here, it's game over."

"So, we have to get Mrs. Olsen here first," Shard said. "She is still your official caseworker and what she says goes. Mrs. Tarantella is just temporary."

"But the problem is Mrs. T is arriving any time now. Even if someone were to convince Mrs. Olsen to come, it'll be six hours there and six back to go get her. We'd never beat Mrs. T up here."

"Too bad we don't know someone with a really fast, sporty motorcycle," Shard said. "And someone who owns one who also happens to be in Whitehorse right now."

"Fiona?" I felt a quiver of adrenalin shoot through me. "Do you think she would help us?"

"She helped you out once before, didn't she? I don't know why, but she seems to have a soft spot for you."

"More likely a guilty conscience. After all, she *is* a Stuckless." I still couldn't forget that her father, Jonah Stuckless, was one of the swindlers who robbed my granddad of his claim. "How do we get a hold of Fiona?"

Shard rolled her eyes. "Are you really the only person in the world who's never heard of a cellphone?"

I just shrugged. My dad and I didn't even have a working toilet, let alone modern electronics. "Doesn't Vinnie have her number?"

"Sure, but he's all the way back in Dawson and too busy to check his phone when he's working. But there's someone closer who probably has her number, and since we don't have one second left to lose . . ."

"You mean Anna? Anna and Fiona can't stand each other!"

"Maybe not, but they both like *you*."

We gave Bullet and the others a quick pat and headed back to the house. Neils and Anna seemed to be deep in conversation when we walked in the door, but then stopped when they saw us.

"I need a favour from Anna," I said. "Well, two actually."

"Sure. What is it?" Anna asked.

"I need you to call Mrs. Olsen and convince her to come up here right away. If she can fast-track the approvals, I won't have to leave." I held my breath.

"You know, he's right," Neils said. "Mrs. Tarantella is only a temporary replacement. Mrs. O has the final say."

"Well, that's great," Anna said. "But Mrs. Olsen is still in Whitehorse."

"That brings me to my second favour," I said, wincing slightly. "Could you call Fiona for me?"

Anna folded her arms. "Anything but that."

"She's the only one who can help," I said. "She's in Whitehorse right now finding a part for Vinnie. With the *Ducati*."

"So?"

"I need her to pick up Mrs. Olsen and get her back here before Mrs. T takes me away."

Anna shook her head and opened her mouth, but nothing came out.

"It's my only chance," I said.

Anna closed her eyes like she was in pain. Then she nodded, took a couple of deep breaths, and dialled a number. "Fiona? It's Anna." Anna walked into the bedroom to have a private conversation. When she came out, she was flushed and rolling her eyes.

"Well?" I asked.

"She'll do it. I'm going to call Mrs. Olsen right now. Hopefully that bike is as fast as Fiona says it is. She sure bragged enough about it."

"What if Mrs. Taran . . . whatever her name is . . . gets to Dawson first?" Shard asked. "We need a Plan B."

I had an idea, but I needed Anna's help a third time and I wasn't sure she'd go along with it. The look on her face when I mentioned it made me think I was right.

"The Ladyhawks are disbanded, Chris," she said. "Even though I want to help you, I doubt the others would be on board. The club ended in a bad way."

"But this could be the difference between me

staying or being shipped off to Whitehorse."

Anna sighed a deep sigh.

"I'll see what I can do."

Shard and I went and sat on the front steps.

"Do you think she can pull it off?" I asked. Shard was better at judging a situation than anyone I knew.

"Come on. Everyone loves Anna. I think they'd do anything for her. That's not the real problem."

My stomach twisted into a knot. "Which is what?"

"Even if Mrs. Olsen gets here first, will she approve your dad? The place is still a mess, and I don't think he's making any money. And with the Filthy Rats still running the show, there's probably some drinking going on. Getting that under control would definitely have been one of CPS's conditions."

Every speck of hope I had just withered up and died. She was right. Things over at the Dearing claim hadn't really improved since Mrs. Olsen was last here. Even if she wanted to help, she probably couldn't.

"I have to go over and talk to my dad."

"I'll go with you," Shard said. "I speak his language."

That's when we heard the sirens.

CHAPTER 23

PRESTO CHANGO

Neils burst out the front door at the sound of the sirens. Shard and I ran to the truck and jumped in, and Neils tore down the laneway. What was going on?

When we got to the end of our lane, we could see two RCMP cruisers turning into the Dearing claim. My heart sank. With one arrest already, it wouldn't take much for the Mounties to believe my dad could be guilty of another crime. Had the Filthy Rats framed him like Shard had predicted?

We followed them down the lane to the cabin. I could hear voices from inside. One Mountie stood by the cruisers.

"Not so fast, young man," he said, catching me by the arm as I tried to bolt past.

"Leave my dad alone," I said, trying to twist out of his grip.

"Just wait a minute, Chris," Neils said. "We don't even know what's going on."

"Hey, Neils," the officer said. "Who's this?"

"Hi, Grant. This is my foster son. His dad lives here," he said, pointing at the cabin.

"Oh, then you should take him home. This is official business."

"I'm not going anywhere until I see my dad," I said.

Just then two more officers came out with the guilty party. Or I should say, "parties," because there were two of them. The Mounties had the Filthy Rats in handcuffs.

Shard and I pushed past the officers and went into the cabin. It was still a mess, but it was empty of people. Where was my dad? Was he okay?

We went back outside, where the officers were putting the Filthy Rats in separate cars. Ballcap and Shifty shot me dirty looks as they ducked into the back seats.

"What's going on?" Neils asked Grant.

"We got a tip these two might be dealing in stolen items. Antiques. When we ran their names, we saw they were wanted for illegally trading in mammoth ivory too. We got them on theft over $5,000."

Neils whistled. "Can't say I'm sorry to see them go. Too many people ignore the laws that are meant to protect our history. What sort of sentence do you get for that kind of conviction?"

"They could be looking at up to ten years behind bars."

I smiled when I heard this. I didn't feel bad for them at all. They *had* stolen my granddad's lamp and scales and they had been dragging my dad down and trying to swindle him. They deserved everything that was coming to them.

The Mounties climbed in their cruisers and backed down the lane.

"I'm going to run you home now," Neils told me.

"But I need to find my dad."

Neils shook his head and ushered me back to the truck. "He could be anywhere. You can't just run wild in the Yukon looking for him. I'll check around if anyone has seen him. You two wait at the house, and I'll call you if I hear anything."

I shook my head. "I'll wait here in case he comes back."

Neils looked unconvinced.

"Shard will stay with me," I added, to reassure him.

I hated waiting. It's excruciating to know your future is on the line and that you're totally helpless to change it. Was Mrs. Olsen on her way? Was Mrs. Tarantella already here?

Would the Ladyhawks be able to help?

"What are you doing? Taking a break?" Shard asked. "We've got work to do."

I snapped out of running all the terrible things that might happen to me in the next few hours through my mind. "What do you mean?"

"Fixing this place up, of course," she said, swatting me on the arm.

"We can't possibly do everything before Mrs. Olsen — or worse, Mrs. T — gets here."

"It's better than doing nothing. You never know what small thing can tip the scale in your favour."

We went inside the cabin and tackled the worst of the mess. After picking up all the dirty clothes and straightening the bedsheets, I noticed sawdust on the covers. I looked up. There were new boards laid across the rafters, making a sort-of loft. I pulled the chair over beside my dad's bed so I could stand on it and see what was up there.

"Is that what I think it is?" Shard asked.

"Uh, what do you think it is?" It just looked like a place to store things to me.

"A loft bed?"

"I guess it could be. With some work."

"Well, what are you waiting for?" Shard said. "Pass me the tools and junk."

So, I did.

"Now, take this second pillow from your dad's bed and this blanket and put it up there. Make it look nice."

Nice? I straightened it out. "But there's no mattress."

"It's a *bed,*" Shard insisted.

"But there's no way to get up there."

Shard sighed and rolled her eyes like the answer was so obvious to her. "There's a wooden ladder outside."

"It's too tall to fit in here."

"So, we cut it!" She marched outside. I followed. She found a handsaw leaning against the bathhouse and grabbed it. I held the ladder while she hacked it off. Then we dragged it back into the cabin and leaned it against the ledge.

"Presto chango. A bed."

This is why Shard was my best friend. She was a girl of action.

We moved on to the bathhouse and did our best to clean it up. We couldn't fix the plumbing, but if no one lifted the toilet seat or turned on any taps, maybe they wouldn't notice it wasn't hooked up.

We heard a motorcycle coming up the lane. I ran out. "Fiona!"

But it wasn't Fiona. It was Vinnie.

He took off his helmet. "I met Neils in town. He said you two were out here, so I've come to take you both home."

"What about the food truck?" Shard asked.

"It's no problem. Business is really slow today. My popcorn kettle is out of commission, but even the muffins aren't moving. I don't know where everyone went!" Vinnie said. "Neils was the only one I saw. He was motoring around Dawson like a man on a mission. What's he up to?"

"Uh, trying to prevent me from being lost in the foster care system forever."

"*That* doesn't sound good," Vinnie said.

"No, it's not. I'm really scared I'll be separated from my dad for good."

"What can I do to help?" he asked.

"I need to find my dad. But I don't know where he is."

Vinnie rubbed his chin. "I think I saw him on York Street, going into the Pioneer Hall."

I didn't even ask if that was a bar; I was pretty sure I knew the answer.

"Can you take me there?"

Vinnie looked from me to Shard. "I've only got one extra helmet."

"I'll stay here and see if I can work on that pile of junk behind the cabin," Shard said.

I shot her a look of thanks, grabbed the spare

helmet, and climbed on behind Vinnie.

We zipped along with the bike backfiring every once in a while, practically giving me a heart attack each time. When we got into Dawson, it was like a ghost town. Vinnie stopped on Front Street by the dike. Just two or three men were walking around, and there were only a few pick-up trucks parked near the General Store.

"Where is everyone?" Vinnie asked out loud.

Then we heard something that sounded like a rumble of thunder. But instead of ending, it kept going and going and getting louder. The ground trembled and shook. Was it an earthquake?

Coming down the highway into Dawson, I saw it: a sea of motorcycles heading our way. The bikes were lined up three across and driving really slowly.

"So *that's* where all my customers are today," Vinnie said.

As they passed by, most gave a wave. I could see that the back of the leather jackets they all wore had a bird with spread wings and a curved beak. Underneath was the name *Ladyhawks*.

"Looks like the old club is back together," Vinnie said. "Fiona told me they broke up about eight years ago and haven't ridden since. Must be something big to bring them together again."

"I guess," I said. I hoped to see Fiona leading

the pack on the Ducati, with Mrs. Olsen on board. But they weren't there. The tide of motorcycles kept coming.

"Where did they all come from?" I asked. "That's more riders than live in Dawson for sure."

"Oh, they are from all around. Some as far away as Mayo."

I spotted a small white car toward the back of the pack, hemmed in on all sides by the motorbikes and forced to crawl along as slow as a tortoise. As it crept by, I saw the driver: Mrs. Tarantella. She was already in Dawson. Where were Fiona and Mrs. Olsen? Mrs. T must have beat them here.

Just then there was a massive explosion a few streets over.

"Fireworks? Today?" I asked. Was there a festival going on that I didn't know about?

"Uh-oh," Vinnie said, looking east to where a column of smoke rose over the buildings. The smoke was thick and black. It looked like it was coming from the spot where Vinnie's muffin truck was usually parked.

"What is it?" I asked, one eye still on the swarm of motorbikes around the car.

"I wonder if I remembered to turn the burner off when I was tinkering with it this morning."

"You go ahead, Vinnie," I said. "I'll find a way

back." I would have to hunt for my dad later. I had to get back to the claim now.

Vinnie looked at the lines of motorcycles, put his pinkies in the sides of his mouth, and whistled. One of the bikes peeled off and rode over to us. When the driver took her helmet off, I saw it was Anna.

"Why aren't you at home?" she asked me.

"I, uh . . ."

"Never mind. Vinnie, can he borrow your spare helmet?"

Vinnie nodded.

"Get on, Chris. I don't know how much longer we can hold up Mrs. Tarantella. And, Vinnie? I have a sinking feeling that blast came from the direction of your truck."

Vinnie paled. "You think so too?" He looked panicked. He climbed on his bike and took off down the street.

I snapped on the helmet and climbed on behind Anna. I had barely grabbed the sides of the bike when she took off to catch up with the group. The wind tore at my shirt as we roared along. Then Anna slowed and swerved up the side of the group, toward the little car. Inside I could see Mrs. Tarantella's face was beet red with anger and frustration. I wanted to giggle but quickly realized that once she got to the claim, she would take that anger and frustration out on my dad and me.

The motorcycles circled Mrs. T's car, trying to slow her down, but she was revving her engine and looked ready to ram through the crowd. Anna motioned to the riders around her to keep up the pressure, but Mrs. T was surging forward and then slamming on the brakes, just missing the bikes nearest to her. I could see the riders getting nervous. The bikes were not coming as close to Mrs. T's car as before, and she was able to move a little faster.

There was still no sign of Fiona and Mrs. Olsen. This was a disaster.

We crept closer and closer to the road that turned off the highway and led to the claim. For a moment there was confusion over who was supposed to block the road, and only one bike turned and stopped, leaving a big gap. This was the opening Mrs. T seemed to be waiting for. The car's motor sprang to life as she swerved around the lone bike and took off down the road. The bikes were in hot pursuit, but it was too late to contain her.

CHAPTER 24

JOB ONE

The choking dust cloud from the motorbikes made it impossible to see anything ahead of us. Maybe that was for the best. Sometimes not being able to see what's coming up makes it easier to keep going.

Finally I could make out that the bikes ahead of us were just idling. We must have arrived, although everything was still hidden by dust. Anna's bike rolled to a stop on the road, beside the lane that led to the cabin. As the dust finally began to settle, Anna and I took off our helmets.

If Mrs. T saw the cabin and claim in that mess from earlier, it was game over for me and my dad. Maybe I could distract her from seeing the worst of it. I jumped off the bike and started running.

"Chris! Come back!" Anna called after me, but I ignored her. This was my last chance.

I ran down the lane, my breath coming in

ragged gasps, and skidded to a stop. Mrs. T's white car was parked by the cabin. The car was empty, and I heard voices inside the cabin. I was too late.

I stood there wondering if I should book it back to Neils and Anna's to start packing for a life on the run or go inside and face the worst.

"Bad news doesn't improve with keeping," my mother used to say. Might as well get it over with.

I pushed open the door and blinked as my eyes adjusted to the dark interior. I almost fell over in surprise. There, sitting on the bed, was Mrs. Olsen. And she was squaring off with a very red-faced Mrs. Tarantella.

"I was brought in to do a job and . . ."

"You were supposed to cover my caseload and maintain my decisions . . ."

"There were irregularities."

"It was a legal and appropriate solution to a very difficult . . ."

"I go by the book . . ."

"You were on a power trip."

You know that feeling when you hear your parents arguing and you want to tiptoe backwards out of the room to escape? Yeah, that's how I felt. I inched back to the doorway and eased my way out. As I walked around the corner of the cabin, I saw the Ducati. At least I think it was the Ducati. It was so caked in mud that it could have been a dirt bike from a motocross race through a swamp.

Fiona had come through. It always surprised me. She didn't strike you as the type you could rely on no matter what, but then people aren't always what they seem.

I found her leaning against a tree just beyond the cabin, texting.

"How'd you get here?" I asked her.

She looked up, annoyed. "Don't you say 'hi' to people?"

"Sorry. Hi." I said. "So, how'd you get here? I was on the highway and you didn't pass me."

Fiona jerked her head toward the back of the claim. "Came the back way, up Hunker Creek Road."

"You must have made good time to beat Mrs. Tarantella."

Fiona stopped texting and gave me a look. "It's a *Ducati*."

"Right. I forgot."

Fiona rolled her eyes. "Shouldn't you be bugging your dad instead of me?" she asked, going back to her phone.

"I don't even know where he is," I said.

"Where he is? He's in the bathhouse."

"Doing what?"

"Well, he's not taking a bath," she said, rolling her eyes again. "He's working like a wild man sweeping up spiders or soldering pipes or something."

Both Mrs. CPSs were still arguing at full volume inside the cabin.

I raced around the back of the cabin. The door to the bathhouse was propped open with a bucket full of green water that smelled like pine trees. I stepped inside. My dad was on his back with his head tilted under the sink. He had a wrench in one hand and was cursing.

"Dad?"

He sat up at the sound of my voice and smacked his head against the underside of the sink. Now he really swore. He rubbed his head and I could see that he had had a haircut recently. And he had shaved too.

"Ow. Chris? I didn't expect to see you."

"I came to see what was going on. What are you doing?"

"Trying to do a few more repairs while those two vultures are distracted by battling it out with each other. I figure every little thing will help."

"Did you hear about those two guys, your partners?"

"Of course I heard. Ian told me what you suspected about my dad's things when I was in the

Trading Post yesterday. I recognized the toe right away. When I went to the RCMP, they checked their database and found those Filthy Rats had outstanding warrants. Then they discovered their trailer was full of stolen loot. I told the Mounties they were also doing the sluice cleanups behind my back. They were robbing me blind."

He went back to tightening a bolt with his wrench, then got up from the floor. "And presto! Running water." He turned the tap and water sputtered for a moment, then came out in a steady stream. "They can't say there is no sanitation now!"

"Wait a minute. You knew they were trying to steal our gold? I didn't think you knew what they were up to."

Dad snorted. "Of course I knew. Not that we found any real amount for them to steal. I've been around enough Filthy Rats in my life not to recognize some when I see them."

"Then why did you let them stay?"

He shrugged. "I needed their money and equipment. And they're kind of too tied up right now to ask for it back for a while." He smiled.

"So why aren't you sluicing?"

"I have something more important to do first."

"What's that?"

My dad stood up, hands on hips. "Get this

place shipshape to get CPS off my back, and you back home, of course."

I froze. I felt my throat closing up and a tightness growing in my chest. Did I hear him right?

There are lots of good feelings in the world: beating a tough level of a video game, eating as much pizza as you want, sailing along behind a dogsled team, laughing so hard your sides hurt. But nothing beats the feeling I had at that moment that I mattered to my dad. I mean, it's something that should be a no-brainer, that you matter to your parents. But you know what? It doesn't always happen, and you spend a lot of time wondering what you could have done differently, or if you could say some magic words that would make them care. But you can't. It's not up to you. And although I spent months telling myself that I would be okay even if no one ever cared, part of me had been empty and sore, like a bruise after you get punched in the arm.

I was cautious, though. I had been let down before.

"Do you think there's a chance?" I asked.

Dad wiped the sweat off his forehead with the tail of his shirt. "Well, the longer they argue, the more I can get done. Hand me that piece of pipe."

"Wait, where's Shard?"

"She's looking for a flange on the old fixtures out back for me."

We were just finishing hooking up water to the tub faucet when I heard the crunch of gravel that was someone walking up the path to the bathhouse. So, who had won the battle inside the cabin? Was Mrs. Olsen giving us another chance or was Mrs. Tarantella coming to drag me away to Whitehorse? If she was, I felt a little trapped in the bathhouse. I braced myself, ready to push past her and make a run for it.

"Tell me that you have running water," a very tired looking Mrs. Olsen said, poking her head in the door.

Dad reached over and turned on the sink tap. Water sputtered out.

"What about the toilet? Tell me the toilet works," she said.

"It's a composting toilet," my dad said. "No water needed."

"Thank heavens," she said, pulling out a clipboard and checking off a box on a long list, "because every detail is going to be scrutinized by a very disgruntled Mrs. Tarantella. Say, is that a *bathtub*?"

"Sure is."

"Well, that certainly helps," Mrs. Olsen said, making another mark on her report.

I stepped outside to face Mrs. Olsen. "Do you mean I can stay in Dawson?"

Shard came out of the bush at that moment holding a small, round piece of metal. "He can stay?" she asked.

Mrs. Olsen shifted her weight from her walking cast to her other leg. "I mean that I have seen some progress with your father. And more importantly, you two seem to have a strong group of people around you who are willing to help support you both." She shifted again. "That's not a small thing, you know. And that has swayed my decision to let Neils and Anna continue fostering you, but also moving to unsupervised visits. If I continue to see improvement, we can talk about you moving to the claim for Christmas," she said.

I looked at my dad and smiled. He tousled my hair.

"Don't get complacent, though," she continued. "Mrs. Tarantella is out to prove herself right and will look for any crack to jump in and get her way. That means stay out of the bars, Frank. I've arranged for you to attend a program. Don't skip it. This can all be undone with one complaint. The agency's mandate is to protect children and they won't sign off on anything unless they're sure."

Dad gave a slight nod. I hoped he understood this was not a done deal.

"And for heaven's sake, get some gold! You need to be making money before I can completely close this file."

She hobbled back down the path, where I could see Neils getting out of Anna's car. Fiona stood by the side of the cabin, arms crossed.

"Thought you might prefer something smoother for the ride back," Neils called to Mrs. Olsen. "You look exhausted."

"That's very kind," she said. "I don't think the bumps on the way up helped my leg any. But . . ." she said, limping over to Fiona and putting a hand lightly on her arm, ". . . that is one fast motorcycle."

Fiona smiled. "You know, we're always looking for new members."

Mrs. Olsen waved off the idea and climbed into the car with Neils.

Dad took one look at how awkwardly Fiona and Anna were acting with each other, then he scooted into the cabin. He obviously didn't want to be around if something flared up between them. I wasn't going anywhere. If a fight broke out, I wanted to see who would win. Fiona was tough, but I think Anna had quicker reflexes.

Fiona and Anna had a stare down. Finally Fiona broke the silence.

"Look, I'd love to sit here and glare all day but I need to relieve my sister of mom-sitting duties before she pops a gasket and starts relabelling all the soup cans just to mess me up."

"I'm not glaring," Anna said. "But . . ." She took a deep breath and seemed to have a hard time getting the words out. ". . . thanks for getting Mrs. Olsen here so fast. It meant a lot."

Now Fiona looked uncomfortable. "Yeah, no problem." She walked over to the Ducati, picked up her helmet, and used a sleeve to wipe the worst of the mud off the visor.

I ran over to her. "Fiona?"

"Yeah."

"I, uh, wanted to thank you too. That's two I owe you now," I said.

"Don't worry, Dirk. I plan on collecting." Fiona looked at Shard. "You need a ride back to town?"

Shard nodded.

With that Fiona gave me a rare smile and snapped on her helmet. Shard put on the spare helmet and gave a wave as they roared down the lane.

A chill went through me. Collect from me, how? She wouldn't make me buy pantyhose for her mother again, would she? Or, with two favours to repay, maybe it would be even worse . . . maybe I'd have to buy old-lady underwear. I started to sweat at the thought of it.

Needing a distraction, I turned toward Anna, who was standing next to her bike.

"I didn't even know you had a motorbike," I said. "I never saw it at the house."

"Yeah, well, I haven't ridden it in a while," she said. "It was under a cover at the back of the garage. Actually, I've kind of missed it."

She climbed on and revved the engine. "I'll be back for you in a couple of hours."

That left my dad and me to work on tidying up the cabin.

For the first time in a while, I really believed it was going to happen — I was going to move back in with my dad. There was just one piece missing: the gold. Without money coming in, we wouldn't survive here.

* * *

We weren't the only ones with money troubles, I found out a few days later. It seemed the insurance company did an assessment of Vinnie's blown-up food truck. Going by its age and condition they had settled on the amount they owed him.

"Twenty-four measly dollars. Can you believe that? Twenty-four dollars wouldn't even fill the gas tank," Vinnie said, when I bumped into him outside the Bonanza Market. I was waiting there for Neils. He had had to make an emergency run into town to buy ant traps for Anna. "First they make me get insurance, and then when something does happen, they won't pay!"

"Didn't you have business insurance?" I asked.

Vinnie looked confused. "I thought because it was a truck, I only had to get vehicle insurance."

When Vinnie's truck exploded, bits of it flew around the neighbourhood. Mr. Bugada pulled the oven door from his fish pond. Vinnie's Muffin Man sign ended up in Miss Fiorenzini's chicken pen. It scared her hens so much they didn't lay eggs for two days. "That sucks, Vinnie. I'm sorry," I said. "What will you do now?"

Please don't say you're going to leave.

"Dunno. I guess anything I want."

"Mom wants to know too," Shard said, coming over to us with a bag of groceries. "She's worried about you."

"Tell my big sister that something will turn up. Something always does." Vinnie headed into the market.

Shard and I started down Second Avenue so I could nip up to the post office. I had promised Neils I'd pick up our mail. We turned onto King Street, and my mouth dropped open as I saw Fiona standing in the middle of the road with another man . . . hugging him. She and the guy went into the Dawson Hotel together.

Shard and I looked at each other. Had Fiona dumped Vinnie? I didn't know what to do.

"Should we tell Vinnie?" I asked.

Shard sighed. "I'll go check on him and see if they had a fight or something."

By the time I got the mail, Neils was waiting for me outside the post office in his truck, so I didn't get to talk to Shard and hear if Vinnie was okay.

It seemed there was less and less to keep Vinnie here. And without him, Shard would have no reason to visit. I didn't want to imagine the possibility of never seeing either of them again.

CHAPTER 25

LOCATION, LOCATION, LOCATION

I went over to the claim every day the next week.

We finally took the burl to Flash Gordon to pay for the bathroom fixtures, and Dad got the sluice plant running again. He was feeding it with dirt from the banks of the creek, where he was sure his father had found the rich pay streak. He showed me how to angle the sluice runs so they were steep enough to remove the dirt and rocks but not so steep that the gold flakes got washed away. He took me up into the excavator with him and showed me how the controls worked. It was the most relaxed and happy I had seen my dad in a long time.

It was almost September and the mining season was on its last legs. Every night it seemed to get colder and colder and there was a heavy frost most mornings. We had to knock some thin ice off the riffles before we could start up the plant.

Dad needed to find some gold before everything froze up. School was starting soon too, and I wouldn't be able to help him as much. He was going to do a cleanup at the end of the week. Washing the mats that caught the gold flakes from the sluice runs was when you got to see the result of all your hard work.

I crossed my fingers, my toes and even my eyes as I stood by to watch my dad pan the concentrate from the mats after five days of sluicing. If Dad was right about Granddad's clue, when he was done, the pan should have a thick layer of golden yellow at the bottom.

My dad was panning over a large bucket so he wouldn't lose any stray grains if his shaking hands slipped and the pan dropped. I held my breath as he got down to the black magnetite in the pan. It always hid the gold, but a few more swirls of the pan should reveal our treasure.

Dad was quiet. That wasn't good. He should be laughing and slapping me on the back; instead he was staring intently into the pan. Finally he looked up.

"Less than an ounce."

I leaned forward to peer into the pan. It couldn't be. Less than an ounce? That wouldn't even pay for the fuel used to run the sluice, let alone our bills over the winter. Neither of us said anything. Dad ran a hand through his hair.

Dad still wasn't talking, so I walked back to Neils's house slowly to give myself more time to think. Something wasn't right. Either my dad had misunderstood Granddad's clue about the gold being in the banks of the creek or . . .? Or what? I got that same niggling feeling I had before. A detail was lodged in my brain and trying desperately to take root.

"Everything okay, Chris?" Anna asked, as I came into the kitchen for supper. I nodded, but inside I was digging. Digging to understand what was bothering me. "Can you get Neils for me and tell him supper is ready?"

I went to Neils's office, but he was on the phone. I waited a moment to catch his eye but he didn't look up. I glanced above his desk at the map of his claim. It was a recent one, not like the historical one in his museum. There were lines drawn all over it showing where they had dug, where the tailings pond had been before it was moved and where roads had been made to get to new parts of the claim. I found the Dearing claim on the map and studied it. I thought back to the old map in the museum. Something was different. My heart skipped. Everything clicked into place. That was it! I knew what was bothering me. I knew why we hadn't found gold on Granddad's claim.

"Supper's ready," I said, when Neils had finished his call. "But I've got to run over to my dad's for a minute." I took off out the door, ignoring Neils calling after me to explain myself. I went the front way this time — no need to sneak over anymore.

I was out of breath when I got to the claim. Dad was nowhere to be seen. I could feel all the excitement drain out of me with the thought that not finding any gold might have made him slip and head into town to a bar. I wandered around for a while, but the mosquitoes found me and started attacking, so I reluctantly walked back to Neils's.

My good news may have come too late to save my dad.

* * *

The next morning I didn't hurry my breakfast. I was avoiding going to the claim. I didn't want to be faced with the reality that I had worked so hard to fix things for nothing. Dragging out breakfast wasn't hard — Anna was a waffle magician. Up until I moved to Dawson, I had only had the frozen ones. Anna made hers from scratch and dusted them with icing sugar before stacking them on a plate.

"So, how was your cleanup yesterday?" Neils asked, slowing down to talk only after he had finished four or five waffles.

"Not so good."

"What are the two of you going to do about it?"

I shrugged. The only thing I could do was check the weather in Whitehorse — because that's where I'd be soon. If only I had understood the problem sooner. If only the Filthy Rats had been caught sooner. If only I wasn't so tired of being hopeful. I should just accept it — the Dearing curse was alive and well.

"I'm going into Dawson," Neils said. "How about I drop you off at the claim?"

I nodded. Neils and I bumped our way down his lane, the main road and then my granddad's lane. Getting out of the truck, I listened for the sound of the sluice running. Nothing.

Neils rapped on the door to the cabin. I paused to see if Dad would answer. Nothing.

I walked to the bathhouse to see if he was in there. Nothing.

"Did he know you were coming?" Neils asked me. Before I could answer, my dad was walking out of the bush, carrying a gold pan.

"Where were you?" I asked.

He held up the pan. "Prospecting. I was testing farther up the creek. I know that gold is here somewhere."

"How did you make out?" Neils asked him.

Dad shook his head.

We all stood quietly.

"Well, I have to be off," Neils said. "Chris, I'll be back before supper to pick you up."

I waved goodbye and walked over to my dad, my eyes locked on him. He had shaved, he wasn't slurring his words and his eyes weren't bloodshot.

"Where were you last night?" I asked. "I came over to tell you something and you weren't here."

His eyes dropped to the ground. "I was at the Pioneer Hall. I had a meeting."

"A meeting? What kind of meeting? The Butter and Cheese Guild? Freemasons? Moose Hunters International?"

"I wish it were the Butter and Cheese Guild. I would join that. No, it was an AA meeting."

"AA?"

"Alcoholics Anonymous. You know, the 'Hi, my name is Frank and I'm an alcoholic' group." He smiled ruefully.

I sucked in my breath. Did he really just admit that? That's what they say the first step is, right? Admitting you have a problem.

"What did you want to tell me?" Dad asked, seeming eager to change the subject.

Right! I had almost forgotten. "I know where the gold is."

Dad gave me one of those *that's really cute but I doubt it* smiles.

"Chris, I was out all morning up and down the creek. It's not there. Maybe your granddad didn't find gold. Maybe he was just hallucinating on his deathbed. And even though he swore for years that those stories of him stealing the dredge gold were lies, maybe it was true after all."

"Yes, he did find gold. I have proof."

Dad tilted his head. "What kind of proof?"

I pulled the nugget out of my pocket. "This. I found it in the cabin rafters by Granddad's toe. Look at the colour. Flash Gordon told me you can tell where gold comes from by its colour. Reddish gold is from the Forty Mile area. His dad knew Granddad's gold wasn't stolen because the gold he tried to sell wasn't full of silver like the gold the dredge was mining. It was reddish, like this."

Dad took the nugget and turned it over in his hand. "What a beauty. But this doesn't mean he found it on *this* claim. Granddad could have found it somewhere else. The gold on this claim is supposed to be in the banks of the creek."

"No, it's from our claim, and it *is* in the banks of the creek, but we've been looking in the wrong place."

"What?"

"The creek was moved."

"Your granddad never said anything about moving a creek."

"Well, someone moved it. Probably before he even got here but he figured it out."

"And how do you know this?"

"Because the old mining map hanging in Neils's museum shows the creek running right down the middle of our claim, not on the border with Neils's property like it is now." I pointed to the east.

Dad said nothing. He just stared.

"Do you want to go to Neils's and have a look at the map?" I asked.

Dad slowly shook his head. "Nope. I trust you. Show me the spot." He grabbed a shovel and a pan.

I practically dragged him across the clearing and into the bush. I searched my memory for the lines on the map and where they should be on the claim.

"Right around here."

Dad studied the ground. He squatted down so he could see the contours of the land under the trees and shrubs. "It does look a bit lower here, like there could have been water flowing at one time." He dug down until he reached gravelly dirt, scooped some into the pan, then took it back to where the creek was now. I stood by while he panned. What if I was wrong? If there was no gold here either, we were done for.

Dad let the water wash the rocks and dirt off

the top of the sample. Then he shook the pan again, letting any of the heavier gold settle to the bottom. The next swishes of water washed away smaller pebbles and sand. He was getting down to the layer of magnetite. As he swirled the black magnetite in the clear water, flashes of gold peeked out from underneath. One more wash and we could see the shimmering layer. It looked like a crescent moon.

Dad looked up at me, wonder in his eyes. "This is it," he whispered. "You found it."

I couldn't speak. The Dearing gold was real.

"Well," Dad said, "what are we waiting for? Let's figure out how to get that ground stripped and the pay dirt back to this plant. There was frost again last night. We have maybe two or three weeks before we're frozen out for the year."

The problem with the old creek bed was that in the years since it was moved, trees and bushes had grown there. We had to clear the area before we could dig up the dirt. Dad climbed into the excavator the Filthy Rats had left behind. He started it and lumbered toward the old creek bed to begin clearing the ground. Because it was so noisy, I didn't hear Vinnie's bike arrive, and I jumped about a metre when Shard came up behind me and tapped me on the shoulder.

"Jeez, Shard. You could warn a guy."

"Here's an idea. How about you CHECK YOUR EMAIL, because I told you we were coming to clean out the garden today."

I sighed deeply. I never remembered email. I looked over to the plot where we had planted the garden. It was a graveyard of brown, limp plants.

"Do we even need to clean it out? Looks like everything died anyway."

"You'd be surprised," Vinnie said, overhearing what I said and sinking his shovel into the ground. He twisted the handle and turned the soil over beside the hole. There were three orange carrots. Then he reached down and pulled on some brown stringy leaves. Up came two garlic bulbs. He dug around some more brown leaves beside them and unearthed a fat onion. It was like magic.

"Don't just stand there," Vinnie said, laughing. "Get me some bowls or baskets or something. We have a *cornucopia* of veggies!"

Shard and I found a couple of fairly clean buckets for the carrots and turnips and some empty cardboard boxes the faucet and bathhouse hardware had come in for the onions and garlic. Vinnie divided the bounty between himself and my dad. It wasn't a whole winter's worth of food by any means, but it was better than having nothing but boxed macaroni and cheese every day.

Vinnie also used scissors to cut off some of the

herb leaves. They had suffered the most from neglect, and there weren't many.

"I think you can keep all of these," I told Vinnie. "Dad doesn't do much fancy cooking."

He piled them on top of the onions and garlic.

"What are you going to do now?" I asked.

"Dunno."

I wondered if he had found out about Fiona and the guy she was hugging? I hadn't had a chance to ask Shard if she spoke to him about it, and she was already sitting on the bike with her helmet snapped on. Vinnie and Shard seemed to have one foot out of Dawson. I wondered if maybe I could talk to Fiona and see if she and Vinnie could patch things up. Who would have thought that I would be wishing for the two of them to be *more* lovey-dovey?

The more I thought about it, though, the more I realized it was unlikely I could change Fiona's mind about anything. She was one tough cookie.

"Well, I hope something comes up," I said to Vinnie, as he carried his veggies to the bike.

"It always does," he replied, with a grin.

I wish I shared his enthusiasm but that's not what happens in my world. Usually when one thing starts going right in my life, everything else goes down the tubes.

CHAPTER 26

A REAL DEARING

"Fourteen ounces," Dad said, holding up the old jam jar with a solid layer of gold in the bottom. He handed it to me. It was heavier than it looked. "Not bad for a week's work."

"No, but I thought it would be more," I said. "Will it be enough?"

Dad laughed. "Enough? That's worth over $26,000." We high-fived and hugged and laughed and high-fived again. "I can finish your bed, get a wood stove installed, and buy some real kitchen appliances. No way Mrs. Olsen will be able to say no to you coming home with all that."

Fourteen ounces would change everything.

But the trouble when everything changed was that *everything* changed. Good and bad. I knew I would probably make a few friends when school started the next week, but I wanted to keep my old friends too. They had stuck with me even when things were tough. You don't find friends like that just anywhere.

That afternoon I asked Anna to drive me into town to say goodbye to Shard. Even if Vinnie did manage to stay, Shard had to go back to school.

As we went to leave, Anna handed me a helmet.

"Are we taking your motorcycle?" I asked.

Anna pulled on her leather jacket and shrugged. "I've missed riding it. Let's go."

Anna's bike was nothing like the smoothness and speed of the Ducati, but I didn't say that to her. There was enough tension between Anna and Fiona; I didn't need to add jealousy to it.

She dropped me off on Sixth Avenue, and I walked to the salmon-coloured house and knocked on the door.

I was surprised to see Shard's mother, Mrs. Kent, answer the door. I guess she had come north to get Shard. Maybe Fiona wasn't heading home yet.

"Oh, hi," I said. "Is Shard here?"

"Well now, Chris. You certainly have filled out. Life up here must be agreeing with you."

I wanted to say that Anna's cooking agreed with me, but instead I just smiled and nodded.

"I'll get Shard," she said.

Shard came to the door, threw on a sweater, and closed the door behind her.

"Come on, let's get away from here."

"What's going on?" I asked, trying to keep up with her.

"Mom and Uncle Vinnie are fighting. And boy, is it a show. I thought it was bad when my sisters went at it, but this is epic. I saw the neighbours closing their shutters and cats running away, ears flat back, to escape the yelling."

"What are they fighting about?"

"Mom says she wants Vinnie to come back with her so she can keep an eye on him. Vinnie insists he's not leaving, and if she wants to keep an eye on him, she's going to have to move up here. She countered with the fact that he's out of a job. He said he has a line on a job and is just waiting for a phone call. She said he's too old to be a hippie. He said she's too young to be an old nag. It got really loud after that."

"So, Fiona isn't taking you back?"

"Oh, that's right. You haven't heard. She bought the Golden Nugget Saloon in the Dawson Hotel."

"She *did*? What about the Bull and Brambles?"

"Sold it to one of the ladies who works there. Lisa, I think her name is."

"Fiona's staying?"

"Yup. That's what she was doing with the guy in the street — buying the bar."

"Is it normal to hug after a business deal?" I asked, still not sure she wasn't dumping Vinnie.

"I think she knew him from when she was a girl."

I was still a bit skeptical. It was funny how protective of Vinnie I had become.

"So, when do you think you're leaving?" I asked.

"Mom wants to head out tomorrow so we'll be back before school starts Tuesday."

We walked along in silence.

"Promise me something," she said.

"Anything."

"Promise me you'll stay in touch."

I sighed. "I promise."

Anna came toward us on her bike.

"Well, see ya," I said. I never was very good at goodbyes.

"Right," Shard said. She wasn't very good at them either. I think both of us were thinking about how weird it was going to be not being at the same school anymore. And sad. Would she make a new best friend and forget all about me? I knew I wouldn't. Shard was one of a kind.

* * *

The next morning I had another look at our claim on the old map in Neils's museum. The creek twisted and curved as it made its way through, so I suggested to my dad that we shift our cut a bit east to better follow its path. Over the weekend I kept busy helping Dad, but by Monday afternoon sluicing was on hold until we uncovered more pay dirt. The first small area he had opened to the east was done. Now Dad was working in the excavator to move the overburden from a bigger section to a pile away from the old creek bed.

The engine revved and roared, filling the air with noise and black smoke. I was taking the mats out of the sluice for a small cleanup. Dad had only run two days' worth of dirt, but with the delay opening new ground, we figured we should start with an empty sluice so we would have an accurate idea of how much gold the ground was producing.

We were both so busy, and the machine so noisy, we didn't hear the trucks pull up. I jumped as the men brushed past me. One went to the control panel of the sluice and disconnected the power. Two others walked over to the excavator. I saw them arguing with my dad, who eventually turned off the machine and got out. One of them hopped in, turned it back on, and began backing it out of the cut and toward the lane — where I could now see they had parked a long flatbed truck.

There was that old, familiar feeling of dread. What now?

I grabbed the last mat and shoved it in the bucket before they began hooking massive chains onto the sluice plant and dragging it to the flatbed too.

"So, that's that, I guess," Dad said, wiping the sweat off his forehead with his sleeve.

"I thought the Filthy Rats were too busy being imprisoned to get their equipment," I said bitterly.

"They are, but apparently the repo guys aren't too busy to take back their machines when the seller realized Daryl and Carl had given him rubber cheques."

"Rubber cheques?"

"They bounced."

We watched them load everything up and slowly rumble down the lane.

"That's the end of our season then, isn't it?" I asked.

"Yup." Dad put an arm around my shoulder. "But don't worry. I'll stretch what we have until spring and then we'll be back in business." He smiled at me, but his eyes looked tired and his smile was strained.

Neils's pickup truck barrelled down the lane.

"What was that?" Neils asked, getting out

and signalling behind him with his thumb.

"Seems my investors forgot to pay their bills."

Neils *hrumpfed*. "Look, it's too late this season, but next spring, talk to me. I know people. There's always someone upsizing, downsizing or leaving the business all together. There's reasonably priced machinery around if you know where to look."

Dad gave half a smile. "I will," he said.

Did I just hear that right? My dad was ready to accept help, and from Neils? A small trickle of real hope seeped into my bones.

After Neils and I headed back, I went to my room to change out of my mining clothes and then got on the computer. Anna was making my favourite — chicken pot pie — as my "last supper" before school started.

But by the time I got to the table, I was too excited to enjoy it. I ate as fast as I could and jumped up from my chair.

"Chris, you're on dish duty," Anna said. "The dishwasher should be full when you add these, so please run it."

"Can I do it later?" I asked. "There's something I have to do in Dawson first. Do you think you could drive me into town, Neils? Please?"

"It's getting pretty late for trips into town."

"It's really important."

Neils looked over at me. "Can't it wait until the morning?"

"No."

He sighed.

We didn't talk much on the drive. I directed him to the salmon-coloured house, then I ran up to the door and knocked.

"Hi," I said, when the door opened. "I just wanted to say to wait for me here tomorrow and we can walk to school together."

There was silence. Then Shard shook her head and laughed. "You're unbelievable. You drove all the way into town to tell me that? You could have phoned. Or emailed."

"I wanted to see for myself that you really were still here."

"How did you know Mom went back without me?"

I smiled. "Vinnie emailed me before dinner. So, your whole family is really moving up here?"

"Mom said it was the only way to keep an eye on her little brother. So, you read your email, eh?" She laughed. "Only took you two months to learn how to do it."

I flushed. "Vinnie also told me he's going to be working for Fiona at the bar. Something about playing a character called Captain MacInnis for the tourists and getting them to drink a shot with a human toe in it? Is that for real?"

"Yup. Was your dad's idea to drum up business. He even donated the toe. That was the ugliest thing I've ever seen."

She didn't have to tell me. "It was my granddad's, you know."

"What was?"

"The toe. I found it in a Mason jar in the cabin. I wonder why Dad didn't want to keep it?"

"For what?" Shard asked. "It's not like he was going to clone your granddad from it. Besides, I think your dad is getting a share of the 'toe tax' they'll charge people."

A bit of money coming in? Granddad saves the day again. With a toe.

"See you tomorrow, then," I said, waving and heading back to the truck.

When we pulled up to Neils and Anna's house, I could see my dad coming down the front steps, a confused look on his face and several containers in his hands. Neils said good night to him and went inside.

"What are you doing here?" I asked him.

"Came to return the chainsaw Neils left at my place."

"What are those?" I asked, pointing at the plastic bowls.

“Anna seems to think I’m starving. She insisted on giving me leftovers.”

I grinned. “If she starts feeding you, you’ll need a bigger belt on your pants soon.”

“Well, I’ll be able to afford one.”

“What do you mean?”

“I cleaned those mats you pulled out of the sluice before they carted it away. Two days, Chris. We’ve only sluiced two days and we had almost twenty ounces. That’s the best ground I’ve ever mined.”

His eyes started to glisten. He put down the containers and gave me a hug. “You are so like your granddad,” he said. “A real Dearing.”

For the first time ever, I was proud to be called that name.

ACKNOWLEDGEMENTS

This book was so much fun to write because every scene reminded me of the amazing time I had when I visited Dawson City and the Klondike. I also have a soft spot for these characters and it was great to continue their story.

Thanks to the whole Scholastic team for their hard work and attention to detail, to Julie McLaughlin for the absolutely amazing cover illustration, to Anne Shone for championing these books, and special thanks to my editor, Erin Haggett, whose enthusiasm and sense of humour made this whole journey enjoyable.

Thanks to Chelsey and Nathan for reading early drafts and never looking bored when I agonized over plot points. Thanks to Alex and Haley for sharing in my excitement. And heartfelt thanks to Craig, who gives me the time and space to write and joins me in the craziest experiences all in the name of research.

ABOUT THE AUTHOR

Natalie Hyde is the acclaimed author of more than seventy fiction and non-fiction books for children, including *Mine!*, *Saving Armpit*, *I Owe You One* and *Cryptic Canada: Unsolved Mysteries from Coast to Coast*.

She lives in Flamborough, Ontario, with her family, a little leopard gecko, and a cat that desperately wants to eat him.